SENTINELS
at the
BLACK GATE

John Eudy

Special thanks to James, Andy, Trina, Dean,
and, as always, my lovely wife, Julie.

Contents

Prelude:
Return of the Anunnaki

The world is no longer in flux. The global war has ended. The viral outbreak, whose origin was never revealed, that ran rampant worldwide did not cause the war. As miserable as the infection made its host, the virus was treatable and only fatal to a small percentage. However, it was at the height of the pandemic that two devastating electromagnetic pulses (EMPs) were detonated. The first was over the northern half of the eastern seaboard of the United States, and the second was over the English Channel. America retaliated against those whom it suspected were the aggressors with its own EMP. Fortunately, a third attack, a digital virus, circumnavigated the globe. The computer virus effectively ended the war by shutting down most computers before it could escalate to nuclear.

However, the damage was done. New York, Los Angeles, London, Moscow, Beijing, Hong Kong, Tokyo, Jerusalem, and nearly all major metropolitan areas descended into chaos. Collapsed power grids, water plant shutdowns, communication blackouts, and halted supply chains fueled the implosion of the world's cities. One-third of the world's population died in the aftermath. Sickness, starvation, and fighting devastated humanity. However, that all ended when the Anunnaki returned.

They did not come to Earth from the heavens, as depicted in ancient texts. Instead, they erupted from the mountains in the American Southwest like ants from a hill that had been kicked. At first, there was panic among the human race as they made their presence known globally. However, they were not aggressive; instead, they offered assistance and peace to a desperate humanity. They provided a new way to generate power, rapidly rebuilt power grids, and reestablished global communications via Artificial Intelligence. Their presence was not only promptly accepted but swiftly embraced.

Physically, the Anunnaki revealed themselves as something different from what antiquity held. A matriarchy, the ant-like humanoid race is tall and slender but with segmented bodies and a small bulbous abdomen where one might find a tail. Most walk upright on two legs but can run on four when necessary. Sharing some similarities to the 'gray aliens' of conspiracy lore, they have acorn-shaped heads tapering to small mouths with slim mandibles and have large, black eyes. Humanity quickly learned that their exoskeletons' color denoted their life station.

Despite their dull gray color, the ruling class of the matriarchy is elegant in their mannerisms. Among the Anunnaki, they alone have two legs, two arms, and two long wings, which drape from their shoulders to the backs of their knees. The working class is tan and wingless. Similarly, soldiers are black but are much fewer in number. They are usually positioned around the queen and governesses or as sentries at colony entrances. Red drones are the only males in the matriarchal race and are rarely seen by humans.

Interestingly, humans with cochlear implants were the first to understand and translate their ancient language. They facilitated communication between the two races. The Anunnaki began co-opting other human technology, starting with Brain-Computer Interface (BCI) chip implants. BCI chips were subsequently connected with cochlear implants and programmed to communicate with Artificial Intelligence (AI) and the Anunnaki hive mind.

Soon after, many, especially military officers and government officials, opted to receive the BCI and cochlear implants for expediency. Those uncomfortable with surgery settled for the non-invasive Ear-Bud Translator (EBT) that fits comfortably over the ear. These translators were paired with a wristop computer. Both could be removed if the wearer wanted to disconnect.

The Anunnaki presence and subsequent technological advancements led world leaders to sign peace accords and unite under the Global Republic of Earth (GRE) banner.

Former nations became 'counties' in the six newly formed continental 'states.' They are Montis Americus Major, Montis Americus Minor, Montis

Europa, Montis Africanus, Montis Asia, and Montis Australis. A human-only penal colony was formed on the seventh continent, Montis Antarcticus. A Governor was elected for each state and paired with an Anunnaki governess. A single human Chancellor was also selected. He resides in the capital city of Denver with the Anunnaki queen, Regina Ravus. Together, they appointed a human warden over Montis Antarcticus.

With a well-established order, the Anunnaki gave humankind the final pieces to quantum computing, cloning, and human augmentation technologies. Humanity lept toward a bright scientific future. This new age of technology, co-existence, and prosperity held the promise of the long-awaited utopia, which was ushered in by establishing a new timeline: Illustratus Aetas.[1] The new timeline replaced the antiquated BCE and AD dates.

Millions abandoned their primitive religions in favor of science and technology. Upon reaching adulthood, most children sought comfortable lives and better careers through these technological advancements. Atheistic Humanism took hold of the world. What is left of the God-fearing is isolated to tiny pockets in Montis Africanus and Montis Americus Minor.

---

[1] "Enlightened Age" – Translated from Latin

Most 'People of the Book' and followers of 'The Way,' as they are called, are minimalized, dismissed, or ignored. Some are used as cheap labor to rebuild ancient pyramidal structures worldwide. However, evangelists from these groups, overt dissenters against the GRE, and those refusing any augmentations found themselves befriending penguins and seals in Montis Antarcticus.

During the first days of Illustratus Aetas, the Anunnaki revealed the existence of a habitable planet in the Milky Way's 3 Kiloparsec (3KPC) arm near the galactic core. They named it Terranaki and designated it as the site of their next colony. They invited humanity to journey there and cohabitate with them. They also reveal a way to get there: a wormhole in the Oort Cloud linking our solar system to the 3KPC arm outside the new planet's solar system.

Using newfound technologies, humankind focuses all its research on this sector. Strange anomalies hovering near the relativistic jets[2] of the supermassive black hole, Sagittarius A*, at the galactic core of the Milky Way were discovered. Evidence of the anomalies is quickly hidden; only a handful have the privilege of knowing. Instead, the promise of space travel and colonizing a planet galvanizes the world's resolve, efforts, and resources.

---

[2] aka plasma or particle jets

The world is no longer in tumult. There is peace and order. In this new age of enlightenment, humankind is on the brink of venturing into space with its ancient alien benefactors. Technological advancements have put the long-anticipated transhuman singularity within grasp, while the promise of exploring a new planet stokes the fires in the hearts and minds of humanity.

Chapter 1:
From Whence They Came

Commander Yared Alemayehu has removed the communication device from his ear and placed it next to him. He sits in blissful silence at the foot of his bed, examining his history and conscience. Tremendous excitement and terrible fear make his heart race.

Different life events slowly transit through his mind. He reflects on his humble beginnings as a boy in Somalia. He remembers immigrating to America as a teenager and joining the Navy as a young man. He also laments the shipmates he lost in the war. He recalls accepting his commission in the GRE Navy and his final transition into the Space Force. Regrets over personal struggles and not starting a family darken his thoughts. They prod his memory toward mistakes made and hurtful acts. However, as a generally positive man, his mind turns to the thrill of his current prospects. It has been a lifelong journey to get to the spaceport in Hagåtña.

"The world I knew in my youth is long gone," he mutters. "We've achieved so much over these last few years. Now, I am afforded the opportunity to travel to a new planet?" He shakes his head and scoffs, "Sometimes, I cannot believe it."

His thoughts drift toward traveling through space with humanity's benefactors and what it will be like. Like a see-saw, worry and fear again counter his positive thoughts. It is not the challenges of space travel or settling on a new world that drive his anxiety. Instead, the cosmic enigma at the galaxy's center dominates his thinking. Black holes are dangerous enough, but the top-secret knowledge of anomalies hovering between the event horizon and the plasma jet perplexes him. The new planet's proximity is close by, too. He wonders if their proximity is a coincidence.

Unexpected teaching from his youth regarding types of angels interrupts his logic. "Could it be?" he asks himself.

An urge he has not felt for many years rises from his heart to his mind. The urge overrides his trust in human achievement and alien technology. Yared is motivated to do something he has not done in decades. Slipping nervously off the bed to his knees, he turns his body to rest his elbows on the bed. He hopes no one will ever discover what he is about to do as it could cost him more than his current assignment.

"Father," he begins. "It's been so long. I have forgotten what to say. I don't know if you would even listen to me after all I have done." He pauses in silence. "However, you know every man's heart and mind and know our needs before we ask. If so, then you know why I speak to you now. Please, Lord, protect me and my crew. Guide us to our destination and make our journey swift and safe."

A rap at his door shakes him from his quiet prayer. He jumps to his feet as the voice on the other side says, "Your shuttle is ready, Commander."

* * * * *

The Anunnaki Queen in her throne room.

Regina Ravus writhes salaciously on her throne in a grand yet secluded chamber within the former N.O.R.A.D.[3] Complex. She is naked, her clothes discarded on the floor around her. Her once-hard gray exoskeleton shimmers a silvery color. Her black eyes gleam, and a sultry smile stretches between her mandibles as she focuses on Kieran, the only human in the room. She slides her hand up from her body to her breasts, tempting him.

Kieran's confidence borders on hubris. He does not feel humbled to be in this situation; instead, he feels he is the best candidate for the job at hand. Every assignment and every career decision was made so he might reach this point. He tells himself he left the Navy because he was bored with the sea and that space was far more exciting, that the lateral to GRE Space Force was for advancement purposes, not to avoid sexual misconduct allegations. *The GRE would not have promoted me if it were not true*, he thinks to himself.

He was positive he was being groomed for a leadership position of substance, a position of significance. *Why else would I be here?* He continues to observe the queen's display while thinking, *I'll be a Captain when I leave. All I must do is impress the queen.*

The queen's scandalous display would repulse most men; Kieran, however, is enthralled and

---

[3] North American Aerospace Defense Command (N.O.R.A.D.) located at Peterson Space Force Base in Colorado

unexpectedly aroused by it. Womanly moans of unknown origin play softly through his cochlear implant. Pornographic images transmitted from his BCI flash in his thoughts. He is an amoral man who abandoned ethical standards long ago, so he does not question where the images and sounds come from nor why the queen's display stimulates him. He is enjoying the arousal.

Regina Ravus' pheromones are overwhelming male drones in the chamber, filling them with a lustful desire to breed. Her male guards drop their stinger spears and begin tearing their uniforms. Flushed with blood, their vermillion shells turn deep maroon.

The queen spreads her wings. A buzz fills the chamber as she flies slowly toward Kieran, who stands on the ornate rug in the middle of the room. Stopping to hover before him, she clicks her mandibles, shakes her abdomen, and moans lasciviously.

Her display is too much for the drones. They swarm toward her. Though he tries to maintain his position physically, Kieran is stomped, cut, and bruised before finally being knocked several feet out of the way. Each male clamors over the other, trying to reach the queen.

Kieran picks himself up and dusts off his disheveled and ripped uniform before observing the violent orgy taking place in the center of the throne room. He marvels with both disgust and an erotic fascination as each male fights to mount the queen.

Regina Ravus lights on the GRE symbol inlaid on the chamber's floor. She allows each drone to penetrate her. Once they provide their seed, she delivers a poisonous sting.

Having expended themselves and suffering from the venom's effects, every drone falls to the floor. Their bodies convulse in a toxic demise.

Once the orgy is finished, the queen stands in the colorless blood of the twitching corpses littering the floor. However, she is not satiated. She steps seductively toward Kieran, "What about you, human?" Her words drip with lust as she turns, bends over, and raises her throbbing abdomen. She looks over her shoulder, asking, "Will you share your seed?"

Driven by an unexplained and depraved desire, he approaches without a word. He loosens his belt. Having witnessed the other males, he places his hand firmly on the shaft of her stinger and presses it against her abdomen before thrusting himself into her.

There is nothing natural about their copulation. It is base and animalistic, a pure show of power and lust. Their unnatural act of fornication is done only to satisfy selfish carnal desires. Primal screams, grunts, and buzzing wings echo in the throne room as they climax.

Panting, sweating, and arching his back, Kieran shoves the queen's abdomen forward. Releasing her stinger and backing away, he has created enough separation to avoid catching his death. Ever watchful of the gray queen, he redresses.

She returns to her throne, picks up her garments, and lazily covers herself. "You have accomplished something no other man or drone has yet." She turns to sit daintily on her throne. Her once lustful smile now appears malevolent. "You survived."

Kieran bows his head with slight arrogance, acknowledging his accomplishment. Though the room is uncomfortably silent, Kieran does not take his eyes off the queen as he finishes tucking in his uniform.

Regina Ravus waits for him to finish before signaling to her servant, who rushes to her side, carrying a folded cloth. She takes it from her. Turning her attention to Kieran, the queen commands, "Come forward."

Kieran hesitates. Undecipherable whispers resonate in his ear implant.

"Do not worry," she says as she stands, her robes hanging off her half-naked form. "You have earned your reward. It is our custom to trade sexual gratification for material gain. You gave me your seed; I give you knowledge, power, and this: an important relic from Earth's past. It was given to us by a great king the last time we helped humanity.

One with such an impeccable military record, which reflects a drive to overcome, succeed, and lead, should be rewarded. I find you are the best human to captain our ship."

Kieran boldly approaches the throne. Regina Ravus unfurls a white baldric with a rather decrepit animal skin sown into it. "This particular baldric," she explains, "is symbolic of the bond we now share. It also belongs to the Captain of my ship. The animal skin sewn into was known to your kind as the 'Clothes of Adam.' You have heard of this artifact, yes?"

"Aye, my queen."

"Good. Then you know the bearer of this baldric is destined to conquer."—again, her grin makes Kieran uneasy—"and we have a grand conquest planned." She invites Kieran forward when she opens the baldric. He moves closer and bows.

"You serve us now," she declares as she places it over his head, "and not that pedantic Chancellor."

Kieran stands and steps back, adjusting the baldric so it fits appropriately across his chest.

"As our new captain, I bestow upon you the name Nimbus."

"Thank you, my queen." Captain Nimbus offers a salute.

"Now, **Captain** Nimbus, go to the spaceport in Hagåtña. We will make all the necessary arrangements for your assumption of command while you await the ship's unveiling. After which, you will receive the final mission briefing … and my offspring."

"Aye, my queen." Nimbus hides his shock at her announcement.

"Do not fret, Captain. We will come for you in due time."

The newly commissioned Captain turns to exit, puzzled by her statements. As Captain of the Bab-ilu and King of Terranaki, he planned for more extraordinary things than 'babysitting' the queen's offspring. Despite the frustration, he is confident and pleased with himself, pleased that his lustful aggression has earned him the power and position he sought.

* * * * *

The doors of the shuttle swoosh open. A female officer sits alone and quiet within. She is slender with jet-black hair properly pinned up in a uniform bun. The young Japanese officer jumps to the position of attention upon viewing Yared's rank.

He raises his hand, "Thank you. Please, as you were."

She waits for him to sit near the pilot's door before returning to her seat. The young woman subtly inspects him as she sits. She notes his name and recognizes him as the Executive Officer or First Mate. She also notices that he wears an EarBud

Translator (EBT) with a wristop[4], a sign that Commander Alemayehu prefers non-invasive augmentation. She quickly turns her head down as he looks in her direction.

Yared introduces himself as the shuttle takes off, "Commander Alemayehu."

"Lieutenant Ibusan, sir."

"Ah, our Bio-tech Officer. I've read your file. Very nice to meet you."

"Likewise, Commander," she responds with a slight blush.

"I understand you are quite brilliant with all these new augments and have been training with MAIa."[5]

"*Arigato*,[6] Sir. MAIa is sometimes hard to keep up with, especially now that she has been paired with quantum computing, but I'm still excited to work with her. I like peering behind the curtain and seeing her inner workings."

"Oh?" He said, politely letting her go on.

"Yes, sir. MAIa, and all AI, does not discern good and evil; she has no so..." Lieutenant Ibusan stops herself. "...emotions. Technically, she cannot lie or tell the truth. She functions on cold, programmable logic."

---

[4] A cell phone-sized, flexible computer screen on a four-inch long wristband.

[5] Name of shipboard Artificial Intelligence
  (Nymph of Greek Mythology and Roman goddess)

[6] "Thank you" – Translated from Japanese

"That a good thing, yes?" asks the Commander.

"*Hai.*[7] It certainly has its merits. Older, non-invasive tech like cell phones were computers integrated with primitive AI but were still helpful. My generation has grown up knowing, living with, and relying on more advanced forms of AI. We're accustomed to it always being there to advise and direct us."

"Are you saying I'm old, Lieutenant?"

Lieutenant Ibusan is instantly flustered. "Oh, no, sir," she stammers. "I just meant."

"It's okay, Lieutenant. I'm just messing with you," the Commander laughs.

Commander Alemayehu looks down at his wristop, "I must admit, I willingly avoid using any AI when making personal or professional decisions. It evolved so rapidly in the last few years, and I'll never pretend to understand how it works. My primary focus these days is to be forward-thinking, anticipating engineering issues, logistics shortfalls, and personnel problems, and that's just to get the ship underway. Anyway, so you believe MAIa is trustworthy and reliable for our journey?"

"*Hai.* She will simplify navigation, efficiently regulate our environment, streamline shipboard operations, especially when we're in cryo-sleep, and make exploration safer for us in general. She might

---

[7] "Yes" – Translated from Japanese

make your job easier if you gave her a chance." She ends with a respectful smile.

"We'll see, Lieutenant. We'll see. You seem to have an excellent grasp of things. I'm sure I'll be visiting you for advice in the future."

Lieutenant Ibusan nods gratefully. Commander Alemayehu looks out the window to see the spaceport nearing.

"Commander?" The Lieutenant asks meekly.

"Please," he says without looking in her direction, "in this informal setting, call me Yared."

Culturally and militarily, she hesitates to address him by his first name.

Noticing the silence, the Commander turns to look at her. He realizes by her bashful expression that he has made her uneasy. "I apologize, Lieutenant. If you're uncomfortable with first names, XO[8] is fine."

She smiles with gratitude. "Sir, I notice you wear the EBT. Based on our mission parameters, may I ask why you did not opt for the implant?"

He grins when he points to the EBT in her ear, "Probably the same reason you did not."

LT Ibusan blushes slightly. "I did not want the operation. I felt bodily autonomy was more important. I also desire to 'unplug' at the end of the day."

---

[8] Acronym for Executive Officer (aka First Mate)

"As did I." He smiles warmly, "Besides, I'm not a fan of needles and scalpels."

The young woman lets a giggle slip past her lips.

"But," Yared continues, "as you said, I've heard about the higher risks without all the augmentations. What is your informed opinion, Miss Ibusan?"

"From my limited understanding of our new ship, I still believe we should be safe without them."

The shuttle pilot's voice interrupts their conversation, "We're approaching the spaceport, Commander. Preparing to land."

"Ah." Commander Alemayehu points to the shuttle cabin and smiles, effectively shutting down the conversation. He turns his thoughts to upcoming meetings and inspections.

The two settle back into their seats as the shuttle descends. Both are pleased with the pilot's gentle docking. The doors swoosh open. Both passengers unbuckle and approach the doors. LT Ibusan gives way for the Commander to step out first.

As they stride across the landing pad, Yared slows and looks over his shoulder at the LT, who walks just behind and to his left. He stops and turns. "Lieutenant, it was a pleasure to meet you. I look forward to your good counsel on this great adventure." Yared extends his hand.

LT Ibusan shakes his hand and then places her hand on her chest, the standard GRE salute. "It will be an honor to serve with you, sir."

The Commander returns her salute, and the two part ways, heading to different destinations in the spaceport.

Chapter 2:
The Bab-ilu

A few days later, Commander Alemayehu is standing on the weather deck of the 110-meter high, cone-shaped Taotaomo'na Pinnacle. The recently constructed pinnacle rises into the sky on Asan Point. Its alabaster color contrasts with the tropical green forests and deep blue sea. Three smaller spires forming a half-circle are built into the hillside behind it.

Taotaomo'na Pinnacle is the primary building for office spaces and technical workshops and serves as the fixed support structure for the soon-to-be-revealed Anunnaki craft. The smaller surrounding spires serve as crew quarters when the ship undergoes upgrades.

Yared stands with the newly appointed Captain Nimbus, Lieutenant Ibusan, other officers, Chiefs, and department heads. They do their best to stay cool under the sweltering, equatorial sun. Fortunately for them, a sea breeze offers some comfort at such a lofty vantage point. From his perch by the extended gantry, Yared can nearly see the whole island. However, he gazes at the deep blue sea beyond the pale blue reef.

He reluctantly turns his eye northward toward the island's air forces and the Enki Ziggurat. The 30-meter-high stone ziggurat in the island's Northwest corner has three stairways. Two lead upward from each corner of its façade, connecting with the primary stairs in front of a central gatehouse in the middle.

Rising from the ziggurat's center is another 15-meter square terrace of steel and glass. This terrace is for socializing, dining, and entertaining. A massive stone pillar runs through the middle of it. Atop the pillar is a penthouse rotunda, which serves as the private quarters for Governors and the Anunnaki ruling class. Four semi-circle balconies surround the dome, making it look like a glittering flower.

Harkening back to the legendary Hanging Gardens, tropical trees, luscious flowers, and vibrant plants surround the glass and steel on the ziggurat's main terrace. Hibiscus, flame, and plumeria trees dot the lush palm trees lining the promenade on all four sides. Multicolored bougainvillea flowers hang over the ziggurat's walls; their fragrance wafts downward on passersby.

A complex of airstrips and landing pads separate the ziggurat from Ravus Air Base on the island's Northeastern tip. Extra security forces have been called down from the island of Tinian to serve as atmospheric escorts. Yared watches various private and military craft continuously take off and land there. From this distance, the air base looks like a bustling beehive.

Turning to his left, Apra Harbor sprawls into the deep blue ocean. Circular docks with white domes float around the outer port like bubbles in the deep blue sea. The harbor was also recently reconstructed and modernized as the premier GRE naval base. Usually, the most advanced ships and submarines are berthed there. However, the harbor is empty today, except for the small security craft patrolling the shoreline. Most of the fleet has been deployed as nautical escorts for the incoming Anunnaki ship.

Looking down into Hagåtña Bay, Yared observes hundreds of civilian onlookers crowding the beach. Thousands of unseen observers stare at monitors inside hotels, shops, homes, and offices. Future crewmembers crowd Taotaomo'na Pinnacle's seaside balconies to witness the Anunnaki ship's approach. No matter their station or place on the island, everyone eagerly awaits the arrival of the Bab-ilu.

Captain Nimbus nudges Commander Alemayehu, "XO, can you believe this place? The Anunnaki have created a techno-oasis in the middle of the Pacific. I'll admit, I marvel at how they've merged ancient stone architecture with technology. The buildings. The port. The air base. It's a tropical jewel, an Earthly paradise."

"Yes, sir. It is gorgeous. Every scientist, technician, and crewmember is truly enjoying their assignment here. Let's hope they still want to leave all this for the mission," he smiles.

"I'm not gonna lie, I'll miss all this," the captain leaned toward Yared, "but only for a little while. I believe we'll build even greater cities where we're going. I'm sure the crew would agree."

Suddenly, an announcement comes over all the monitors through implants and translation devices. "Our esteemed Cancellarii, Regina Ravus, wishes to address the world."

Her image appears on every monitor, screen, and wristop. Regina Ravus' voice is heard in millions of thoughts and ears. "Citizens of the GRE, my friends. Today is a great day. One to surpass all those before it. For this day, we share our ship and mission with you. Our coexistence and unity these past years have led to a near utopia here on Earth. But the time has come for some of us to leave this paradise. To venture into space and colonize a new planet. To build a new civilization as one people."

The officers and crew on the support structure can hear applause erupt from all over the island.

Regina Ravus breaks for the applause before continuing, "We have often been asked why we chose to reveal ourselves in mountainous, arid, land-locked regions and hid our ship in the Marianas Trench. We did so because we wished to keep any fear of our return to a minimum. We discerned that a public, highly visible aerial arrival would instill greater panic across the globe. So, we chose discretion, hoping it would lead to the unity we currently enjoy.

With our shared spaceport in Hagåtña Bay complete, the time has finally come to present our ship. We are proud to give you the Bab-ilu."

Her image is reduced to an inset while the wider video feed shows the massive ship slowly breaking the ocean's surface several miles south of Guam. Sea water cascades from its dark metallic surface. As it rises into the air, its tubular shape is revealed. Two curved plates, one above and one below, run the length of the cylindrical center. Various shapes form the superstructure, which runs the length of it between the upper and lower shields. Water pours from the openings at each end of the tube-like craft while a giant ring spins rapidly around the ship's center. Water evaporates into steam around the spinning ring.

"Our star-bound city likely does not evoke the sleekness you might expect based on humanity's fictional craft or from your historical rockets and shuttles. However, its interstellar and wormhole capabilities make up for what it lacks in appearance."

Witnesses on Guam 'ooh' and 'ahh' as the ship rises and approaches.

"I am sure that by now, you have noticed the massive spinning ring at midship. In addition to creating a magnetic field to shield against interstellar radiation and space debris, it also generates gravity within the ship. MAIa, our ship's artificial intelligence, safely manages the gravitational field. Rest assured, the field will be dampened while the Bab-ilu is in port for safety. It will be fully energized when the time comes to escape Earth's gravity."

While Regina Ravus informs the populous, a young technician standing with a gaping mouth close to the gantry on Taotaomo'na Pinnacle mutters, "Hours of research, writing reports, calculating probabilities…" His voice trails off momentarily before continuing, "None of it compares to all this. To being here … now. We witnessed the solution to the Fermi paradox when they arrived, and now, we're about to overcome the final hurdle of the Great Filter theory with this new ship. It's like a fantasy fulfilled." His logic and reason give way to childlike wonder as he bounces slightly with glee.

Yared glances over his shoulder in time to see the security chief elbow the technician. "Get grip, man," he whispers in a Russian accent. "And for f***sake, wipe zat tear off your face."

Yared laughs silently at the Chief's response.

Regina Ravus' broadcast continues, "…MAIa uses quantum computing to calculate multiple navigational routes through the galaxy and gravity-based technology to steer; the Bab-ilu's propulsion system is based on particle fusion. You'll soon notice the rings on either end of the ship. Material is collected and fused to generate a gravity well. Once the weight of the fused material reaches its proper mass, it is ejected. Using a human term, this 'sling-shots' us through space at incredible speeds."

"That is a quick summary of the ship's technical abilities. As for accommodations for our fearless human crewmembers, they will find the Bab-ilu very comfortable. Suitable dining halls, observation decks, and private quarters will be retro-fitted into the superstructure on either side of the ship. Engineering and Anunnakian quarters will remain above and below the twin hulls."

The cameras cut to the officers and technicians on the support structure. "Speaking of our daring crew"—drone cameras pan their faces as she speaks—"I am proud to give you Captain Nimbus. A decorated and respected GRE leader, he hails from Montis Americus Major. We are confident he will lead the crew safely to our shared destination."

Captain Nimbus offered a salute with a slight bow to show gratitude and humility.

"His first mate, Commander Alemayehu, who hails from Montis Africanus, will ensure adherence to GRE core values, a safe and expedited voyage, and mission completion."

Yared similarly salutes.

She goes on to introduce other officers, both human and Anunnaki. Each one follows their captain's example. Afterward, the camera refocuses on Regina Ravus.

"Tomorrow," she says, "your newly selected crew will begin renovations and training with MAIa." She pauses briefly to allow some clapping.

"In closing, my fellow citizens, we, Anunnaki, are once again happy to offer our technology to humanity, and we look forward to this unprecedented joint endeavor. May it bear much fruit."

Applause and cheering erupt all over the island. Regina Ravus nods her gratitude, and then the camera shifts to the incoming Bab-ilu.

The cheers fade to hushed awe as the massive ship slowly navigates around the island to dock at the Taotaomo'na Pinnacle. Everyone watches in amazement as machines connect and gangways extend. Afterward, a buzz fills the air atop Taotaomo'na Pinnacle as crewmembers, technicians, and citizens flood aboard, excitedly chattering.

* * * * *

Later that evening, Yared approaches a table in the dining hall with a tray in hand. "May I sit with you, Chief?"

"I'm not best company, but khey, you're XO, you can sit vherever you like, Commander." His Russian accent is ripe with sarcasm.

Yared sets his tray on the table but continues to stand. "Is that how you address a superior officer, Chief?"

"Superior? Pfft." Chief Orlov takes a drink, then wipes his lips with the back of his hand.

Yared leans forward, resting the knuckles of his fists on the table. He scowls at the Chief, who shoves his seat from behind him as he stands. Onlookers stare in uncertainty.

Chief Orlov tilts his head slightly and gives the Commander a hard look. However, he cannot hold it for long. He laughs out loud. "Khow've you been, *tovarishch*?"[9]

Commander Alemayehu stands upright, laughs, and extends his hand. "I'm great, you salty dog. And you?"

Chief Orlov clasps his friend's hand and gives it a good shake.

Realizing there will never be an altercation, the other diners return to their meals.

"Please, sir." He motions to the chair. "I vould be khonored to dine vis you." The two sit together.

Yared picks over his food with a fork. "So, CHIEF Orlov now, huh? What're you, 30? And you've already earned the anchor."

"*Da*."[10]

____

[9] "Comrade/friend" – Translated from Russian
[10] "Yes" – Translated from Russian

"It's been a long time since our days on the GRS VENTURE." Yared pauses to reflect briefly. "You were an outstanding operator."

"And you vere good Lieutenant—all zose boardings. We never failed our mission or lost anyone, did we? Khere you are, First Mate, on ship headingk into uncharted territory? You've come long way, too."

"And you. Starboard Security Chief has a nice ring to it."

"*Spasibo*.[11] It does. I've got starboard side; Chief Byrd khas port side. Ve'll keep you safe, Commander."

"I was thrilled when I saw your name on the crew roster, Aleksander. I look forward to your good counsel … Chief." Yared's tone changes slightly. "By the way, did you really need to be so harsh on that tech in the glass room?" He asks with a chuckle.

"*Da*. Khe deserved it. Lost his military bearingk and needed gentle reminder. Khe'll get over it."

"You get home to Vladivostok before coming to Guam?"

"*Da*. Enjoyed seafood vis old friends, gave away all my stuff, except few personal effects, of course, and visited parent's graves to say final farewell," admits Aleksandr. "I'm ready for voyage."

"Good. Good." Yared realizes that their food is getting cold. "I'm sorry. Please, eat."

---

[11] "Thank you" – Translated from Russian.

The two dine together without a word. Although Yared is glad to see his friend and shipmate, knowledge of the anomalies slips into his forethoughts, and he becomes visibly distracted.

Aleksander finishes his meal, places his dinnerware on his tray, and pushes it toward the middle of the table. "Your soughts, Commander?" He asks.

"Oh, it's nothing."

"Come now, Commander. It's been vhile, but I can see somesingk distracts you."

Yared looks around. He hesitates before leaning forward to quietly admit to his friend, "I've been questioning many things lately, especially my beliefs."

"Beliefs? Like vheser or not aliens exist?" He chuckles.

"No, Aleksandr. I've been thinking about The Way."

"Pfft." Aleksandr waves his hand dismissively. Out of respect for his shipmate, he keeps a low tone when he replies, "No one believes zose archaic religions anymore, sir. Ve khave freedom from religion now. Besides, most who cling to zhose ideas are shovelingk snow. Maybe zhose ancient alien whackos vere right. Look at all ze sings khumanity created once ve stopped believingk in God."– Aleksandr makes the quote signs with his fingers when he says–"Khe doesn't 'provide for us.' Not only khave ve created technology to provide for ourselves, but ve're about to rocket into space with zose same ancient aliens."

"Indeed." Yared pauses. "Chief, what level of security clearance do you have?"

"Clandestine. Same as you."

"Right." Yared again looks around before continuing, "Come on. I want to discuss something with you in private."

Aleksandr follows Yared, dropping off their plates on the way out of the mess hall. They stroll into the central passageway and head for the balcony near the crew's quarters, which faces the spaceport. They can see the Bab-ilu moored to the service structure.

They look around the observation deck to make sure they are alone. Leaning over the railing, Yared confides in his trusted friend about his briefing on the anomalies at the galaxy's center. "They're like black asterisks against the white plasma of the particle jets. They don't move; they defy all laws of gravity."

"And...?" Chief Orlov states, "It's probably radiological interference, remnant of collapsingk star, or somesingk."

As they're speaking, Lieutenant Ibusan silently passes the balcony entrance. She hears Commander Alemayehu's voice and slows. Intrigued by their discussion, she pauses on the other side of the wall by the entrance to listen.

"No. My instincts tell me they're something greater. If I may confide in you, Aleksandr"–he hesitates–"An old religious lesson from my youth plagues me. I can't get it out of my head that the anomalies are of divine origin. Nothing from the material world could resist those kinds of gravitational forces."

"Divine? Vhat do you sink zey are?"

"I know this may sound crazy, but my hunch is these anomalies are beings, not organic nature or inanimate material. I think they're Cherubim. What I can't figure out is what they're doing hovering around the black hole at the center of our galaxy."

"Cherubim. Like ze chubby little angels vis tiny wings? Khow can you tell zat from khere?"

"No, no. I mean the four-winged angels with four heads from ancient biblical times."

"Bah. You're imaginingk zings, Commander. Cherubim were said to guard Tree of Life in Eden, but we never found Eden or zem."

"Yes, well, call it a gut feeling based on the data I read in the briefing." Afterward, Yared whispers, "Sometimes I wonder if they still guard it."

"Khuh?"

"Oh, nothing." Yared pauses before admitting, "I'm just beginning to wonder if our true mission is settling a new world or if there is a hidden mission revolving around these anomalies. I can't shake the feeling we're being misled."

"I singk you khave nervous jitters. After all, ve are about to travel interstellar space on one-vay trip. Once ve're out zere, you'll see more accurate data firsthand and forget about ancient religious stuff."

Regret enters Yared's mind. He feels like he has said too much. "You're probably right, Chief. It'll be good to have you around to keep me even-keeled."

"*Da*, Commander. I'm khappy to be your soundingk board." He stands upright, places his hands on the railing, and says, "Ve've got lot of learningk to do startingk tomorrow. I'm gonna valk around facilities before khittingk rack." Aleksandr extends his hand. "It's pleasure to serve under your command again."

Yared shakes his friend's hand. "Thanks, Chief, and good night." He then leans over the railing and returns to staring at the Bab-ilu.

LT Ibusan turns and moves silently down the corridor before Chief Orlov discovers her. Intuition tells her there is more to the Commander's theory. She decides to keep a close eye on him and Chief Orlov.

Aleksander stops in the entryway to look back at his First Mate. Doubt and worry enter his mind. He hopes he'll never have to place his shipmate in shackles as a dissident.

* * * * *

The next day, Commander Alemayehu introduces Captain Nimbus to the assembled crew.

Nimbus addresses the crew at an all-hands assembly. He tells them how excited he is to have such skilled and talented shipmates. He restates their mission, that they're about to embark on a once-in-a-lifetime opportunity to colonize a new planet. He also reminds them this is a one-way trip and that there will be no return to Earth. He encourages them to train hard and to say their final farewells to loved ones.

Afterward, the Captain meets with Yared and other lead officers. He knows Commander Alemayehu's service record and speaks highly of him. He conveys confidence in his First Mate and encourages all the officers to place their trust in him as well. Having the confidence of the Captain pleases Yared and should make his job as XO a little easier.

However, a little while later, during a private discussion on the pinnacle's weather deck, Yared picks up on a trait in the Captain that might make his job more difficult. He notices the Captain ogling female technicians coming and going from the Bab-ilu—some smile back at him, but most stay focused on their task.

To 'feel out' his new Captain's motivations, Yared disguises his concern when he questions, "Captain, I'm sure you're aware that because it's a 'one-way' trip, every crewmember selected for this voyage is single. I hope to keep personal relationship drama to a minimum. What are your thoughts?"

"As XO, I expect you to do so. However, it is a long voyage, and I expect there will be some shenanigans behind closed doors. I doubt we'll see any inter-species breeding. However, as we get close to our objective, I expect coupling or pairing off among the officer corps to occur naturally. There's likely to be some straight-up fornication among the enlisted crew, too. You know how they are. Either way, we'll need to populate the new world, so I don't plan on suppressing it as we get closer to our destination."

Just then, three enlisted crewmembers walk by. They offer a salute and greeting, which Captain Nimbus returns. He stares at the female in the group as though he were undressing her with his eyes.

After she passes by, he says, "Who knows? I might even engage in a little 'cross-pollination' myself. Won't you?"

"Actually, Captain, my goal is to get us there safely first, make sure we can survive, and then I'll consider starting a family."

Nimbus straightens, saying, "And I would expect nothing less from my XO. Now, if you'll excuse me, Yared, I see my drones approaching. I'm meeting with security before visiting the Anunnaki spaces."

"Aye, Captain." Yared salutes and departs. He knows he has a new challenge before him.

Over the next few weeks, the charismatic Nimbus will freely walk through the shoreside facilities and the Bab-ilu. He is gregarious and open when he speaks with the crew, getting to know them and kindling an expeditionary excitement among them. He builds trust with the Anunnaki and encourages teamwork, inspiring the entire crew.

* * * * *

Three months later, the human facilities are finished, training is complete, and the ship is fully stocked with all the necessary materials. The crew is beyond excited to depart. Commander Alemayehu is exhausted from coordinating supplies, resolving minor personnel issues, and studying shipboard operations. At this point, he feels more relief than joy that everything is ready for the voyage.

Regina Ravus quietly arrives at the spaceport without her human counterpart, the GRE Chancellor. Unaccompanied, she discreetly travels to the ziggurat the night before she is to deliver the great commission. Rumors swirl in quiet corners that Captain Nimbus was invited to the penthouse rotunda for more than a final mission briefing.

The next day, all off-duty human crewmembers are assembled at the nearby airstrip while the Anunnaki crewmembers form up on both sides of the central ziggurat steps. Senior human officers and key Anunnaki crewmembers mingle and dine in the reception terrace. Media drones circle the ziggurat rotunda, awaiting the emergence of Regina Ravus.

Appearing on the balcony in the late morning, she emerges with an unknown Anunnaki from the ruling class before the day's heat. Both are elegantly dressed and face the crew below. The circling cameras take positions around the balcony to broadcast her speech globally.

"Citizens of our great republic, my friends," she greets as usual. "The day we have worked so diligently toward has finally arrived. Today, as a unified people, we set our eyes on a new world and prepare for departure."

A thunderous applause erupts from the crowds in Hagåtña.

She continues, "In ancient times, we welcomed humanity into our underground colonies so we might survive turbulent periods on Earth's surface. Later, when times were bountiful, we raised our mounds, pyramids, and monolithic structures skyward on almost every continent."

"Thanks to our shared technology, we will not just build monuments here, but we will lose the bonds of Earth and travel to a new world where we will build a whole new terrestrial paradise with even greater wonders."

Once more, she pauses for mass praise from an adoring crowd.

"By the time the intrepid Bab-ilu reaches Terranaki, MAla will have perfected cloning and digital assimilation. With this new technology, we will grow new augmented bodies and upload our consciousness into them. Death will no longer hold sway over any of us. Instead, it will become optional."

"Once our unified Terranaki colony is established, we will connect our two civilizations, sharing resources and technological advancements. We will have eternal prosperity and utopian peace."

The crowd erupts in applause. As they do, Regina Ravus steps to the side while her counterpart glides forward.

The queen raises her hand toward her, saying, "As a symbol of commitment to our symbiotic unity, I present to you my daughter, Ishtar. As I once did, the time has come for her to leave the mound and establish a new colony on Terranaki. Ishtar is the perfect vassal. She will fly into the unknown with you,"–Regina Ravus gestures toward the ship's crew–"the heroic crew of the Bab-ilu."

"Fortunately, Ishtar will never have to search for a suitable companion as I did, for she will have the daring Captain Nimbus at her side." Regina Ravus turns to welcome Captain Nimbus as he strides confidently onto the balcony to much fanfare, especially from his crew.

Nimbus, who once thought he would be a caretaker for some spoiled Anunnaki child, has instead learned Ishtar is a lovely young Anunnaki female. He graciously salutes Regina Ravus before offering his hand to Princess Ishtar, who accepts it daintily. Together, they stand side by side at the balcony railing.

The Bab-ilu crew cheers for their captain and princess, as does everyone else watching the ceremony.

Regin Ravus concludes, "Let us celebrate this momentous occasion with a global feast day! For tomorrow, we reach into the heart of the heavens."

Thunderous applause initiates worldwide celebrations. Parties, festivals, feasts, and revelry last hours on every continent … everywhere except Montis Antarcticus.

Chapter 3:
Into the Heavens

It has only been two months since the Bab-ilu slipped the bonds of Earth. The artificial gravity makes everyone feel like they're on a cruise ship at sea. Only there is no horizon, and the sea of stars and celestial bodies is far more brilliant outside Earth's atmosphere. As promised, the Anunnakian ship travels at superior speeds, too. She passed the red planet only days ago on her way to the Asteroid Belt.

MAIa has accommodated everyone's needs, making life in space safer than expected and far more enjoyable. Furthermore, with their extra appendages, the Anunnaki have proven invaluable as helmsmen and navigators. It has been an excellent start to a long voyage across space and time. Everyone is looking forward to what speeds the Bab-ilu's fusion drive can achieve.

The asteroid belt, a magnetically neutral area between the sun and Jupiter, was designated as the ideal location for creating a gravity well. It holds plenty of material for the fusion engine, and any debris left behind should be safely captured by Jupiter's gravity, preventing it from moving toward Earth.

As they approach the asteroid belt, Nimbus sits at the helm instead of his captain's chair. As Captain, he is obligated and sincerely wants to pilot the ship on this occasion. The additional pride of being the first human to activate Bab-ilu's fusion reactors also motivates him.

Princess Ishtar stands behind his captain's chair, observing. Thus far, she has displayed a stoic presence with a light-handed approach in her interactions with the crew, placing herself subordinate to Captain Nimbus. Currently, she watches Nimbus and the bridge crew closely.

Captain Nimbus eyes a cluster of minor, pock-marked asteroids drifting above the rest of the belt. Slowing the ship, he guides it toward the patch of space rock while simultaneously lining up the ship with her future trajectory. The bridge crew holds their collective breath as the Bab-ilu drifts closer and closer to its objective.

Commander Alemayehu, who has taken a position at the nearby control panel, informs, "Captain, MAIa reports the cluster is mostly C-type[12] asteroids, but there are some M-type readings as well. The cluster you have selected is perfect for our needs."

"Excellent. XO, notify the crew to prepare for collection."

"Aye, Captain." Yared flicks the intercom switch, "All hands, prepare for material collection."

"On my mark, Commander," Nimbus directs.

---

[12] Carbonaceous or "C-type" and Metallic or "M-type" asteroids

He guides the ship to the precise spot, lining up the intake bow with the cluster. Then, he fires small booster rockets, bringing the Bab-ilu to a complete stop. Satisfied with his abilities, he sits back, ordering, "Engage."

Commander Alemayehu conveys his order over shipboard comms, "Initialize fusion."

"I'm turning over navigational controls to MAIa." Captain Nimbus sets the controls before motioning for the duty helmsman to return to his post.

A new, low-frequency humming sound begins to reverberate through the Bab-ilu. Everyone on the bridge watches as the asteroid cluster funnels toward the ship. There are no collision sounds or alarms as the space debris enters the ship's core, just a steady hum as each asteroid is sucked into the fusion chamber like space ice into a straw.

Nimbus returns to his captain's chair. Ishtar slides over to stand just behind the right side of him when he sits. She places her hand on his shoulder, acknowledging him.

"XO, monitor gravity readings and let me know when we can purge fused material," Nimbus commands.

"Aye, sir."

Other than muted operational communications and the clicks and beeps of the control panels, there is general silence on the bridge. The crew watches random loose asteroids streak across the ship's magnetosphere while waiting patiently for the fusion collider to collect its material. The cyclical purring of the collider gradually speeds up as the last of the space rock is siphoned in.

Yared observes the physical compression of the material and sensory data of the density of the mass on his monitor. It doesn't take long for the fused mass to develop gravity as it is compressed. It's mere minutes when he reports, "We're nearly at critical mass, Captain."

"MAIa, confirm navigation coordinates and prepare to expel mass."

A computer voice responds, "Coordinates set for Kuiper Belt, Captain. Countdown to launch initiated." MAIa counts down in a robotic Latin, "Decem, novem, octō…"

Nimbus recalls his youth when he took delight in knocking birds out of trees with a slingshot. He instinctively clutches the arms of his chair, expecting major g-forces. Smiling, he quips, "I guess we're gonna find out what it's like to be the rock in a slingshot, huh?"

Most of the human bridge crew follow his example.

The princess giggles. "I assure you all; you may relax. The Bab-ilu will buffer any gravitational forces. You will not feel a thing."

MAIa's digital female voice continues the countdown: "… tria, duo, ūnum. Launch."

A muffled 'whoomp' sound, like material blown out of a cylinder, signifies the expulsion of fused material. The spaceship is immediately thrust into space at incredible speed. Small asteroids bounce off the magnetic field, creating a fantastic but short-lived meteoric shower.

There are no g-forces; no crewmember is thrown back in their seat. All the humans on the bridge look around at each other.

Ishtar smiles. "See, you did not feel a thing."

"Hmpf," Nimbus grunts. He secretly wanted to feel the rush that comes with a rocket-fueled launch.

Yared turns his chair back toward the monitors and checks the readings. "Incredible!"

"What is it, XO."

"We're traveling at over ten million kilometers per hour."

"Any reports of damage or malfunctions," inquires Captain Nimbus.

"No, sir. Everything is functioning as normal," responds Commander Alemayehu.

Captain Nimbus pats his armrests and then presses the intercom button. "Well done, crew! Successful launch. We are traveling faster than any human has before. This is history in the making!"

Cheering pervades the whole ship.

Captain Nimbus lets the cheers die before announcing, "We will reach interstellar space in a few weeks. We are going deeper into the heavens than any human ever thought possible. To celebrate, shipboard liberty is hereby granted for all non-essential duty personnel."

The crew's enthusiasm is elevated as they are propelled toward the end of the solar system and beyond.

* * * * *

Weeks later, a tired XO sits in a dark corner of the observation deck. He comes here often to decompress from the day's duties. The quiet spot provides a place to reflect on his daily decisions and directions. Genuinely pleased with the crew's performance and high morale, Commander Alemayehu initially lets his thoughts settle upon humanity's future on Terranaki.

An increasingly contemplative man, his thoughts dwell on more practical, material concerns that MAIa has not been able to answer. Such ponderings as, *Will there be life on Terranaki? Will there be animals to hunt for food or domesticate? Will the soil accept Earthly vegetables, or will there already be eatable ones? How long will we have to live off the ship's greenhouses? Will there be material to construct our homes and towns with? Or will we need to deconstruct the Bab-ilu to build our city?*

He reassures himself that Earthly explorers and colonizers had the same fears and concerns, and most were successful. Subsequent thoughts of

Christian colonists direct his thoughts toward The Way.

It seems barreling through the darkness of space and time toward an unknown landscape can cause a man to question his beliefs. From Hagåtña to now, his once-forgotten faith has been rekindled. Sitting quietly, barely noticing the planetary wonder passing by, Yared reflects on how often tenants of The Way have influenced his choices and directions. Total secularism and superficial human materialism have slowly become secondary in his operational decisions. He wonders if decisions based on faith are suitable for the crew.

Suddenly, a whisper from an unfamiliar voice fuels the secret doubt in his mind, "What if your destination is not Terranaki? What if your destination is darkness and gnashing of teeth?"

These two unexpected questions echo through his mind, derailing his philosophical and practical train of thought. He returns to his intuition that the anomalies might be actual angels; *as far-fetched as that sounds*, he thinks.

All these questions lead Yared to think about his past life choices. He recalls all the 'dumb things' he did in his youth. More than a handful of regrets from his days rounding up dissenters creep up on him, especially the memory of unloading prisoners at the Montis Antarcticus facility.

A final idea pricks his conscience: *Can I be forgiven?*

Preoccupied by deep thoughts, Yared has not only been distracted from noticing the gorgeous blue hue of Neptune passing slowly by but also rendered oblivious to his immediate surroundings.

"Good evening, Commander," greets a soft female voice.

Startled from his contemplation, Yared glances over at the young Miss Ibusan. "Oh, hello, Lieutenant."

"I'm pleasantly surprised to find you here," she says.

"This is a good spot to unwind, is it not?"

"Yes, sir, it is. It's just … I thought you had a window in your private quarters."

"No. I don't, unfortunately. Even if I did, I would likely come here for a wider window and better view of Neptune." He watches her remove her EBT, attach it to her wristop, and deactivate both. "Off going, I assume."

"Yes, sir. May I?" She gestures to the chair beside the table.

"Certainly," he says before returning to the view. "Breathtaking, isn't it?"

The gently sloping walls lead their attention through the rectangular portal to the azure Neptune rotating in its 165-year orbit. Supersonic winds drive the dark blue storm in Neptune's northern hemisphere while small white clouds streak across other parts of its atmosphere. Light from the distant sun illuminates tiny moons while faint rings crown the planet. The planet's vivid blue set against black space is like a sapphire on a black velvet cloth, dusted with tiny sparkling diamond-like stars. They are calmed and mesmerized by it.

After a long and happy silence, Mitsuki says, "I cannot believe I'm sitting here, watching the furthest planet from the sun drift by as though it was an everyday sight. No human has ever seen Neptune with their own eyes. Yet, here we are, freely traveling the stars to establish a colony on a distant planet. I never imagined it would happen in my lifetime. Did you?"

"Of course." Yared chuckles.

Mitsuki takes her eyes off Neptune to look at Commander Alemayehu with great curiosity.

"You see? When I was a boy in Africa, I would stare up at the radial arm of the Milky Way stretching across the night sky. I often identified planets and constellations, but sometimes, I would lean back on a boulder and imagine I was flying a rocket ship through space. 'Course I was sitting in a cockpit with thrusters on full, blasting through the cosmos, stars whizzing by. No time to casually observe the furthest planet in our solar system." He smiles at Mitsuki, who lets a giggle slip out.

"Very funny, Commander," she says sarcastically before gazing back at the blue planet. "You know what I meant."

"I do, but I enjoy your smile." He, too, turns to observe the passing planet. "Truly, this journey has been amazing … and it's only just begun."

"*Hai,*" is all she says in response.

Yared admits, "I have spent a fair amount of time on the observation decks since we catapulted past Jupiter. Usually, when no one else is around. Though my job keeps me busy, the vastness of space is never lost on me; always something new to see out here."

"Each planet does seem more vibrant out here," Mitsuki offers.

Because Yared feels calm and trusts his company, he does not think when he says, "There is so much order and beauty to creation. I have trouble believing it is all here by chance."

There is an extended silence before Mitsuki leans toward him, whispering, "Creation denotes a creator, Commander."

"Yes, well, what I meant was…" Yared stammers.

"It's okay." She casually looks around, ensuring no one is close enough to hear her. Still, she speaks softly, "You can speak about those things with me. I was raised by followers of The Way on the island of Kyushu."

"Oh," Yared whispers. He pauses to consider what she just admitted.

"*Hai.* My Sobo, my grandmother, was sad when I stopped attending Mass. She thought I lost my way."

"Have you?" He asks quietly.

"Let's say I walk a parallel path. I try to keep the narrow path in sight."

Yared remains silent momentarily before admitting, "Sometimes I feel like I, too, have lost my way, Mitsuki. Lately, however, a voice has been calling me back to it." He raises his finger toward her, "But that is strictly between you and me. Yes?"

"*Hai.*"

"Hmm," acknowledges Yared—the two return to observing Neptune in silence, contemplating creation and the secret they now share. Although Mitsuki and Yared's friendship began soon after the launch, a deeper bond, a trust, formed between them.

* * * * *

The Bab-ilu decelerates after passing Neptune. Before navigating past the Kuiper Belt, it has a side mission: to position satellite relays on the inner and outer rings. Radiation and interference from other celestial bodies have degraded the quality of transmissions from Earth. For the most part, MAIa's algorithms have compensated, but the relays will boost signal strength.

MAIa designates a safe orbit for the first relay away from Neptune's gravitational pull and out of Pluto's elliptical orbital path. These relays were prepped before launch and do not require assistance from the crew to place in orbit. MAIa deposits the first relay like a lonely sea turtle before returning to the sea.

Afterward, the Bab-ilu collects a small amount of asteroids and generates another gravity well. One powerful enough to send them quickly over the extended icy donut that is the Kuiper Belt, but not into interstellar space. On the outer edge of the belt, a twin relay is deposited. Each satellite is loaded with additional sensors and will collect more in-depth data for future voyages.

A greater quantity of space debris is collected from the outer edge of the belt for the launch into interstellar space, where the solar winds begin to dissipate. The secondary fusion thrusts the Bab-ilu toward the heliospheric edge and into interstellar headwinds.

* * * * *

Despite the satellite relays, comms with Earth are still strained and sporadic as they navigate through the hydrogen wall. Soon after they cross the bow shock and enter interstellar space, the Bab-ilu receives an unexpected transmission from Earth. Due to the message's classification, only Captain Nimbus and Commander Alemayehu are privy to the recording. The two sit in a secure transmission room with locked doors.

The XO presses the play button, and the message begins, "Greetings, Captain Nimbus. I apologize for the lack of formality, but a serious problem has developed on Earth that may impact your journey. Ophiocordyceps unilateralis, commonly known as zombie-ant fungus, has jumped species and infected the Anunnaki. We have yet to discover the source of the infection. Unfortunately, it overtook Regina Ravus."

Commander Alemayehu pauses the message, looks at Captain Nimbus, and asks, "Do you recognize that voice?"

"No. Do you?"

Yared shakes his head 'no.' He returns to playing it.

The message continues, "Video footage from within the now quarantined N.O.R.A.D. compound shows the Anunnaki queen stumbling through the passageway leading to her throne room. She was heard repeating, 'Time to go. Time to go.' The last camera captured her stammering, 'Must get to Oort Cloud.'" There is a static break in the recording.

Nimbus and Yared glance at each other with concern before the recorded message crackles back to life, "After fighting through rabid worker drones, human inspectors found the queen clutching the pinnacle of the ceiling in her throne room. She had dug her fingers, toes, and even her mandibles into the highest beam. A large Cordyceps fungus had grown out of her head. Corpses littered the throne room floor. Everyone was accounted for except the guards. None of them can be found. We strongly advise testing your Anunnaki crew for the Cordyceps fungus. If you find it…" The transmission ends abruptly in static.

Yared turns off the playback.

Captain Nimbus asks, "Do you know anything about this fungus?"

"I have heard of it before. If memory serves, the fungus takes over an ant's body and drives it toward high ground, the underside of a leaf, a branch, or something similar where it latches on. The ant is dead before reaching its destination, but the fungus drives it on. That's why it's referred to as the 'zombie fungus.' Once it's there, the fungus digests the ant's innards. When finished, the fungus grows a mushroom-like plume out of the ant's head or thorax and rains down pollen, infecting others."

"Ugh! That's disgusting."

"I agree, Captain. It's gruesome."

There is a brief silence in the room as they contemplate the possibility of widespread infection on the Bab-ilu. Having been in that throne room, Nimbus imagines what the horrific scene there might have looked like. He knows certain fungi can grow on human tissue, which makes a more profound concern creep into his thoughts.

Finally, Captain Nimbus breaks the quiet, "Yared, despite our current technology, I lack confidence in clear communications with Earth. Based on how that transmission ended, I'd say we're not going to receive any further details before we reach the wormhole, either."

"Agreed, Captain. In the meantime, may I recommend we direct Lieutenant Ibusan to work with MAIa to search for irregularities in our Anunnaki shipmates? She might be able to uncover signs of infection through their implants. If not, I'll look into conducting ship-wide testing using something non-invasive like saliva."

"That sounds good. Get her on it ASAP and report to me with your findings." Nimbus starts toward the door. "We need to ensure this fungus is not on the Bab-ilu. We cannot afford a mass infection among the Anunnaki or let it jump species and afflict humanity."

"Captain?"

"Yes?"

Yared asks nervously, "Do you intend on informing Princess Ishtar? That is, should we get her consent or help to inform her people?"

"Not yet. The last thing I want to do is cause panic among the Anunnaki or alarm the rest of the crew. Work with Lieutenant Ibusan and develop the saliva testing privately. I want to keep this between us for now, XO."

"Aye, Captain."

* * * * *

Despite galactic forces pushing against it, the Bab-ilu still travels at incredible speeds toward the Oort Cloud. Everything is running smoothly and quietly. Engineering checks, wormhole preparations, logistics, and security rounds preoccupy the crew with a subdued routine.

Almost everyone on the Bab-ilu has experienced extended periods underway on ships at sea, but this is different. There are no port calls in foreign lands. Out here, there is no sunrise or sunset, no moon reflecting off the ocean surface. There is no rise or fall of the tide or choppy seas. No exotic foods or markets. Just months of slow and steady traveling. It's beginning to wear down the crew. Yared dubs the awkward feeling 'circadian malaise.'

The observation decks are frequently empty since there is nothing to see but blackness and distant stars. This leads many crewmembers to seek comfort and pleasure in each other. Not so for Commander Alemayehu and Lieutenant Ibusan. They have more pressing concerns.

With their translators in their pockets and wristops turned off, the two officers dine together in an empty mess hall. Yared knows cameras are everywhere, and he knows MAIa monitors them all. He tells Mitsuki to eat while they talk, which disguises their conversation.

The Commander informs Mitsuki of the possibility of infection. He directs, "I need you to work with MAIa to develop a discreet algorithm to detect traces of the Cordyceps fungus in the Anunnaki. I can't stress this enough, Lieutenant; it must be discreet. I don't want to raise alarms or attract unnecessary attention with these initial scans."

"I can do that, XO. They have an augment in their exoskeletons that monitors vital signs. I'll start there and see if irregularities appear." She suddenly silences herself.

Looking over Yared's shoulder, she sees Chief Orlov enter the dining hall with a food packet.

Chief Orlov brings strolls up to their table and asks, "Commander. Lieutenant. May I join you?"

"Please." Yared motions to the empty spot at the table. "I'm glad you're here, actually. I need your security insight." The Commander also motions for him to remove and turn off his EBT and wristop.

Aleksandr sits, complies with the Commander's directives, and then begins eating while Yared catches him up on the topic. He also explains why they're eating and talking at the same time.

"Chief, I'm going to develop protocols for saliva tests. In your experience working with the Anunnaki, do you foresee resistance to this kind of testing?"

"*Nyet.*[13] Sure, zere'll be one or two disgruntled Anunnaki who dislike being tested by humans, but I

---

[13] "No" – Translated from Russian

singk majority vill understand zis is for health and safety."

"That's acceptable. So, we have a plan forming. Good."

"So, Mitsuki, do you still feel the same as the day we met regarding MAIa and humans merging with machines?"

"To a point. AI is still beneficial and good ... as long as it is not manipulated to distort hard facts. MAIa has done well in helping us get this far."

Yared lifts his cup to his mouth and asks, "And augmentation?"

"Although I prefer the non-invasive type, I must admit, I am curious how human and technological evolution will advance on Terranaki. I hope humanity is not lost in the machine."

"*Da*. I agree." Aleksandr inserts, crumbs falling from his mouth, "Ve don't need planet of Frankenstein's monsters."

The Commander chokes on his drink and laughs at the Chief's boldness. "Seriously, Aleksandr?"

"Vhat? I'm just sayingk. Between body devouringk fungus, demented AI, and invasive tech augments, ze last singk ve need on new planet are mindless brutes vis tech stickingk out of exoskeletons runningk amok."

Mitsuki lowers her head slightly and covers the grin on her face.

Yared shakes his head. "That's why I love having you on this ship, Chief; your unfiltered candor."

* * * * *

What would have taken hundreds of years in the past is accomplished in mere months when the Bab-ilu reached the Oort Cloud. The observation decks fill up with non-essential personnel for the first time since passing Jupiter. Everyone wants to see the rocky bubble surrounding the solar system with their own eyes. Strangely, neither Captain Nimbus nor Princess Ishtar are present on the bridge. Commander Alemayehu has assumed control during this event.

The wall of icy space debris comes slowly into view. At first, it reminds human crewmembers of the high, wispy cirrus clouds. As the ship draws nearer, the asteroids forming the spherical shell are more reminiscent of the bumpy cirrocumulus clouds in Earth's atmosphere. However, this 'cloud' is not made of water vapor. Shadowy, pockmarked asteroids the size of mountains and sometimes larger lurk in the darkness.

The Bab-ilu decelerates to scan for the wormhole. As it does, an object smaller than a dwarf planet but more extensive than an asteroid moves downward, exposing the hidden blue and purple hues spiraling around the black gateway. Frozen dust and debris encircling the wormhole shimmer among the ultra-violet lights.

MAIa announces that the final research and communications satellite has been positioned. It will take readings and observe the Oort Cloud and wormhole. Humanity has researched and confirmed many interstellar objects and their properties, but until now, wormholes have always been hypothetical. Yared and others on the bridge scan their monitors for the satellite's first readings.

Only those on the bridge or forward observation decks can see what's coming. MAIa provides data, measurements, and scenarios using advanced sensors to ease concerns. Still, the swirling ultraviolet portal unnerves many human crew members, including Commander Alemayehu.

Princess Ishtar can feel the rise in anxiety through the hive mind. To assuage their fears, she addresses the entire crew from her private quarters, "Let me reassure you, my friends, the wormhole may look formidable, but simply put, it is a stable tunnel through the dark matter of space. Like our earthly tunnels, we Anunnaki have built passageways through space and time. I reassure you it is safe."

"Our rate of travel will only be accelerated in time, meaning there is nothing to fear regarding the Bab-ilu's structural integrity. She is truly space-worthy. Navigating the wormhole will be quick and safe. There will be a deceleration upon exiting, similar to what we experienced exiting the heliosphere. That slowing should allow us to get our bearings, adjust our course, and reach our destination safely."

The silence onboard is notable when she pauses. The whole crew hangs on her warm and delicate voice.

"Thank you all for your hard work and dedication. The journey thus far has been a joy for me, and I look forward to your reaction when we arrive at our destination. Now, I give you your captain, who has further instructions."

"Thank you, Princess Ishtar," he begins. "As you know, it will still take approximately one year to pass completely through the wormhole. That is a relatively short amount of time, considering the vastness of space/time we're crossing."

"Now, I know the circadian malaise is starting to affect us all. MAIa has established alternating six and nine-month cryogenic and duty cycles. These hibernation cycles depend on your rank and station and will go into effect soon after we enter the wormhole. Cryo-sleep will help time pass easier and allow everyone to rest ahead of our primary mission. We will complete the rest of the journey with a minimal but effective crew. Scheduling questions should be directed to your supervisors, department leaders, or MAIa."

Ishtar saunters toward her bed, which causes Nimbus to temporarily click the microphone off. He watches her intently as she moves toward the bed.

He clicks it back on, broadcasting, "That is all for now."

Nimbus shuts off the ship's intercom and turns his chair away from the console. Ishtar is sitting at the foot of her bed with her legs crossed. She is leaning back on her arms. He is unashamed when eyeing her.

She knows that look but acts innocent when she inquires, "What are you thinking, my Captain?"

"Innuendo, my lovely Ishtar."

"Pray tell, what innuendo?" Her tone softens to a teasing one.

Nimbus alludes, "Don't tell me the idea of this long, hard shaft of a spacecraft entering the wormhole is lost on you. Personally, it makes me consider something other than space travel."

"Oh?" Ishtar tilts her head and lets her dress slip off her shoulder. "And what might that be?" She asks, seductively leaning to one side and curling her legs on the bed. Her dress strap falls a little lower.

"We are to be Chancellor and Queen of Terranaki, yes?" Nimbus asks.

"Of course, my darling captain."

Nimbus approaches her. He runs his hand down her shoulder, sliding the dress down further until her breast is nearly exposed. "Maybe we should consummate our relationship as future rulers."

"Mother directed me to give myself to you when right." She rises to meet Nimbus, letting her dress fall below her breasts. She whispers, "Maybe the time is right."

Nimbus places his hands on her sides, slowly moving them upward.

"Mother said having you was very satisfying."

"She did?" He smiles lustfully. He cups her exposed breast. He leans in to kiss her thin neck. "That was work, my dear. Being with you will be pure pleasure."

Chapter 4:
Wormhole Visions

The crew breathed a sigh of relief when the Bab-ilu entered the wormhole without incident. Comfortable with the warp-like travel speed and tired of the circadian malaise, most crewmembers immediately sought their cryogenic cycles. Many were hoping for a nine-month rest. While the crew looked for rest, Nimbus was looking to leave.

Nimbus had gotten out of bed and was getting dressed. He took a moment to gaze down at his latest conquest. Ishtar slips the covers up over her naked body. He watches the sheets ripple as her body glides underneath. She raises her head, then resting on one hand, props her body up. She is staring at him with those cold, black eyes. It's then that he notices something odd. Her silvery color is losing its luster.

He touches her bare arm, asking, "Your skin is changing color. Are you okay?"

Ishtar pulls her arm away, "I'm fine. The color change is normal after we breed for the first time."

Her bitter tone takes Nimbus by surprise. Most of his other lovers, especially those he has deflowered, beckon him back to bed. This time feels far more transactional. He is not offended by the change in tone. Instead, he finds it refreshing; he believes there will be no need to make excuses to leave. Knowing he was the first to have Ishtar is also incredibly satisfying.

He sits in a nearby chair to put his boots on. When he does, Ishtar sits upright in bed, covering herself with the sheet.

"We need to discuss the so-called anomalies, Captain," she states with an unnerving grin.

* * * * *

Chief Orlov and Lieutenant Ibusan are scheduled to enter cryo-sleep soon after the Bab-ilu establishes wormhole stability. Aleksandr is relieved by his counterpart, Chief Byrd, who will lead security for the whole ship while Aleksandr hibernates. They will switch places six months into the journey. Mitsuki is slated to enter cryo-sleep two weeks after Aleksandr but will not be woken for nine months.

Yared meets privately with Mitsuki and Aleksandr in a secure room to discuss the Cordyceps testing before they go into cryostasis. A part of him feels like this fungus is a distraction, something to take his focus off Terranki and the black hole anomalies. Unfortunately, he can't risk setting testing aside.

"I've been monitoring rhythms in Anunnaki vital signs, Commander. I have found no abnormal measures," Mitsuki reports.

Aleksandr reported that he did some digging and inspected security personnel rosters. "None of ze Anunnaki served at N.O.R.A.D. facilities, sir."

"Right. Well, that's all a relief." Yared sighed. "Still, I'll develop protocols for random saliva testing while you're both asleep. Mitsuki, I'll need you to develop a device for sample collection before you go into hibernation. After the protocols are finished, I'll work with medical to establish culture testing. We'll have MAIa track the cultures and provide results." He pauses briefly. "If we do this right, the test might be useful for unknown issues once we reach Terranaki."

"Chief, I'll need you to provide a light security presence during sample collection. I want to ensure everyone's confidence in the process, especially any reluctant Anunnaki. Plus, I'll be asleep when the Lieutenant begins testing, and she might need a hand collecting samples."

Aleksandr asks, "Vhat about Princess Ishtar? Is she to be tested?"

"I'll speak with the captain on that. I'm sure he'll want to be the one who breaks the news to her and asks for a sample."

"Aye, sir."

"Lieutenant, are you good?"

"*Hai.*"

"Excellent. I expect you'll both do a great job. Thank you."

* * * * *

It isn't long before Chief Orlov checks in at the Cryogenics Wing. Though security concerns have been minimal, the long trip through space has taken its toll; he feels exhausted. Unfortunately, the development of the saliva-testing device keeps the Lieutenant from seeing Chief Orlov into hibernation. However, Yared is there for him.

Aleksandr sits on the edge of the stainless steel tube while a Cryo Tech finishes connecting all the necessary electrodes and sensors.

Standing at the foot of the cryo-tube, Yared asks, "You ready for this?"

"*Da*, Commander. I sleep like Russian bear in winter."

Yared chuckles, then says, "I need to ask a favor."

"Anysingk you need, sir."

"Will you keep a watchful eye on Mitsuki when you wake? She's going to need a guardian angel," he says.

"I'm no angel, Commander, but I vill keep her safe," Aleksandr confirms.

"Thank you, Aleksandr. I know you will, my friend. I know you will."

The tech finishes his work, and Aleksandr slides on his back into the cryo-tube. He adjusts his body until he's comfortable. Yared closes the cylindrical cover and then moves to the foot of the tube. The tech seals the tube and begins the cryogenics procedure. Yared stands by until he knows his friend is safely in hibernation.

A few days later, Lieutenant Ibusan delivers her prototype saliva collector to the Commander on the same day she's scheduled for cryo-sleep. He is impressed with her creativity and rapid results. She informs him that MAIa can also easily replicate the device in large quantities.

He thanks her for her hard work, and as with Chief Orlov, Yared also stands by her as she enters hibernation.

* * * * *

Elsewhere, in the princess' darkened quarters, Ishtar tosses and turns on her bed. Her body flinches, and her antennae twitch. A multi-layered voice echoes in her head. It tells her, "You have done well, my daughter, but it is time for us to take over. You must give us control."

She wakes and sits up in bed, "It was all a dream," she mumbles.

"It is no dream," the callous voice booms in her mind.

Ishtar knows her mother's voice when she hears it. She answers her through the hive mind, "I let the human have his way with me as you wish. Does this please you, Mother?"

"It does, indeed, my servant. However, we have greater plans than seduction. The time has come for you to give in to us so that we may accomplish our goals. You must let us rule."

"If you would only tell me, I could…"

"NO!" The brutal voice shrieks in her mind.

Ishtar knows further questioning will bring only pain.

A softer voice persuades, "You agreed to be our vessel, child. However, since you desire to see the fruits of your labor, I will allow you to remain with me in spirit once I have control. Now, it is time for you to relinquish your body to me. I am and will be the queen."

"Yes, Mother," Ishtar agrees. She accepts her role in this mission and complies without further resistance.

Ishtar lays back in bed, readying herself for spiritual possession. She spreads her arms outward and straightens her body. Once she's in the position of a cross, she clears her thoughts. Her head and hands begin to twitch at first before shaking violently. She unconsciously sits up and spreads her wings. They flap awkwardly at first but soon start humming, elevating her seemingly lifeless body above her bed. Her flinching limbs drop still, hanging at her sides. Her twitching antennae droop forward. The room grows nearly as cold as the space outside. Her exoskeleton fades to a darker gray.

Suddenly, her arms and legs stiffen outwardly like an 'X.' A vicious smile spreads across her face, and she chitters in a multi-layered demonic voice, "There. That is better. Thank you, my daughter."

* * * * *

Yared finds solace in the observation deck after his friends and confidants go into hibernation. Though they're no replacement for a good sunrise or sunset, at least the wormhole lights change. The variant colors outside contrast the sterile, artificial white lights illuminating the ship's interior. Sometimes, the wormhole lights are spinning; sometimes, they appear almost liquid. At best, they're mind-numbing. At worst, they're hypnotic. Either way, daily mundane problems dissolve, and his mind turns toward more serious developments: a growing divide between humans and aliens.

It started when word got out that the Anunnaki crew was to be tested for the Cordyceps fungus. He can't confirm it, but he suspects the princess communicated the plan through their hive mind. He thinks this because Captain Nimbus informed him that he had spoken to Ishtar, and she decreed that there would be no Cordyceps testing. She assured Nimbus that all infected Anunnaki were left behind on Earth. The Captain, of course, believed her.

Yared wonders if Nimbus betrayed his confidence and spoke to Ishtar immediately after the secret communication or if MAIa informed the princess. Either way, he no longer believes that what he says in confidence will stay confidential.

He rubs his forehead to ease his mind. He wishes Mitsuki or Aleksandr would pop in so he would have someone to confide in, but he is alone with his thoughts, which unexpectedly turn to his childhood faith.

There was a simple peace when he was a boy, happiness in following his parents in The Way. He hopes he can return to that life on Terranaki. It is a new beginning, after all. Perhaps he can retreat to a quiet corner of the world and live as he did as a boy in Montis Africanus.

He finds a small measure of happiness in thoughts of faith and family. His headache recedes.

* * * * *

Nimbus leans forward in his captain's chair on the bridge. He's sulking over Ishtar's recent chastisement of his relations with another Anunnaki female. Ever since he took her virginity, she has turned bitter and resentful. He justifies fornicating with other women because she has no love for him.

Then, he mutters, "It's the hive mind. That's how she found out. I'll have to stick to human women from now on." His arrogance grows daily.

The gears turn fast in the mind of the once bold, decisive, and benevolent captain. Putting aside his lust, he ponders what Ishtar told him about the anomalies. He never believed in spiritual things growing up. Believing in Heaven or Hell was for the weak-minded. However, if the Cherubim do exist, if they are actual creatures, he thinks hunting them down might bring him glory in the eyes of his crew. He knows the ship is armed with Anunnaki weaponry, and if that doesn't work, the fusion core could strike the celestial beings down.

"Imagine the power and prestige if I could accomplish such a task," he whispers.

He sits upright and begins to plot and plan.

* * * * *

Days later, Captain Nimbus grants a private meeting with his XO. The two meet in a rarely used forward observation deck. It's a small room in the Anunnaki section of the ship above the intake. This room is limited to higher-ranking personnel and offers a spectacular view of the entire tubular wormhole ahead of them.

Yared sits behind a small table. When the door swooshes open, he jumps to his feet.

"As you were," Nimbus says. He gestures to the control panel, "Mind if I lower the shield?"

"No, sir."

"Thanks. Those spiraling lights have been giving me a headache lately." He pushes a button on the control panel next to the door. The metal shields close over the half-circle portal, and the room's lights change to a soft but bright yellow. He then strolls over and sits in one of the two more comfortable chairs facing the front of the ship—Nimbus motions for Yared to join him.

Yared sits in the chair next to him.

"Unless something's changed, XO, I know we haven't received further communications from Earth. So, why the request for a private meeting?"

"First, thank you for meeting me here, Captain. I know you have more important things on your plate now, so I'll be quick and frank. Since word of the proposed cordyceps testing got out, I've heard whispers of corruption and growing mistrust in the Anunnaki. I'm also hearing rumors of an alternate 'mission' to bypass Terranaki to hunt down celestial beings at the black hole." He gauges Nimbus' response, but the captain remains silent and stoic.

"Sir, may I speak freely?"

"Don't you always, Yared."

"I know this is completely off-topic, but I feel like something changed after we entered this wormhole. I suspect an evil presence on this ship; something wicked is driving us to a terrible end."

"Bah! That's just your primitive superstitious mind," Nimbus waives his hand dismissively.

"Okay. That may be the case, but will you at least address my mission concerns, Captain? Is there an alternate objective? And do you think Princess Ishtar might be hiding insurrectionist thoughts in her people?"

"Do you genuinely believe I would allow mutiny on my ship, Commander? I am becoming a giant among men and Anunnaki alike. None would turn on me. And, if there were an alternate mission, don't you think you would know about it? Even if there were a mission to hunt down alien beings, we would complete the mission."–Nimbus unconsciously tugs at his fur-adorned baldric–"I am unconquerable. I will not allow anything to happen to my crew."

"Sir, with all due respect, only your ego has grown to gigantic proportions. I've seen how you've come to treat your crew. Your objectification of everything and everyone is becoming a concern. You see everyone and everything as a means to an end, **your** desired end."

"You forget your place, Commander. This is my ship. We will go where I direct, and you will follow orders or be relieved of your duties."

Captain Nimbus stands. Out of respect, Yared does as well.

"XO, your concerns, petty as they are, are duly noted. I'll let you know if I choose a different mission." He points his finger at Yared. "And I will expect you to accomplish it," Nimbus threatens before storming out of the room.

* * * * *

The Bab-ilu is halfway to their destination when Yared enters hibernation. He is slated to be revived two weeks before the Bab-ilu exits the wormhole. Chief Orlov, who came out of his cryo-sleep a few days earlier, is standing by his friend when he safely enters cryostasis.

Captain Nimbus enters the cryogenics facility after Yared is asleep. He stands next to Chief Orlov and looks down on his XO. After a short silence, he orders, "Chief, I want you to place a guard nearby. We need to keep watch on this one."–he taps the outer shell of the cryo-pod–"I fear space madness may be infecting his mind."

Nimbus turns to face Aleksandr. "He will have no nano-med assistance[14] or stem cell resources while in cryostasis. Understood?"

"*Da*, Captain."

Nimbus returns his attention to Yared's cryo-pod. He says in a hushed tone, "I want him weaker. I want him to fear his death and embrace the transhuman faith when he wakes."

Aleksandr sees the apparent divide between his Captain and XO. He doesn't know what caused it, but there is a noticeable change in Captain Nimbus' demeanor. He recalls a similar mentality and rhetoric from his days on the GRS VENTURE. It was directed toward followers of The Way then. He

---

[14] Microscopic nanorobots (nanites) are injected into the bloodstream to repair and maintain bodily tissues and organs, especially in cryogenics.

wonders if Yared has become more devoted to The Way, and the Captain moves to persecute him.

Though he privately questions the orders, Aleksandr follows them. He immediately assigns a guard and then informs medical regarding the Captain's directives for Commander Alemayehu.

Chief Orlov spends the next two days catching up on security concerns and reacquainting himself with the ship and crew. He enjoys a daily sparing session with human and Anunnaki security personnel to regain his strength. In doing so, he notices that the Anunnaki have become more aggressive and violent than they used to be. He wonders if extended space travel is adversely affecting them.

He often travels the low-lit gray metal corridors, which seem smaller. Their curved walls with rib-like supports from the flat metal deck to the flat overhead make him feel as though he is in the gullet of some interstellar leviathan. He feels almost out of place as he makes security rounds but chalks it up to hibernation effects.

Aleksander also notices a strange, hushed paganism spreading on the ship, reminiscent of ancient Greko-Roman practices. Furthermore, What was once expeditionary excitement among a united crew has morphed into the selfish pursuit of personal pleasure.

On one occasion, he turned down a relatively quiet passageway only to find two female crewmembers kissing passionately outside the door to one of their quarters. They stop when he draws closer. The women display no shame or embarrassment. Instead, one of them lustfully invites, "You want to join us, Chief?"

Aleksandr's heart begins to beat faster—his face flushes. The temptation to join in is strong. If only for a second, he imagines being with both of them. Murmuring, salacious moans fill his EBT, fueling his lust. "Indulge your deepest desires," a voice whispers faintly in his ear. His right hand begins to shake slightly; he wants to reach for them.

Then he remembers there are cameras everywhere. He quickly snaps out of the pleasurable thoughts. He knows a younger version of him would never have hesitated. However, as he matured, he learned enough self-discipline to control his urges. Chief Orlov values his rank, position, and reputation far more than a fleeting moment of self-indulgence.

"*Nyet*. I don't singk I vill, ladies," he says, slightly shaking his head.

The one with her back to the bulkhead reaches for the door panel while the other unzips her uniform and slides her hand inside. She moans when the door opens, saying, "Your loss."

The two slip into their quarters, quickly closing the door behind them.

Chief Orlov's heart rate slows, and his hand stops shaking. "Vhat was I sinkingk?" he mutters.

He hears more of the same happening behind closed doors in human and Anunnaki quarters as he wanders the ship's passageways. Contemplating why there is so much sexual activity, he concludes that MAIa has made the journey so easy and comfortable that many crewmembers have turned to selfish pleasure instead of working.

He suddenly stops and pulls the EBT out of his ear. He recalls the sultry voice in his ear. Staring at it suspiciously, he asks himself, "Is MAIa influencingk our bekhavior?"

He hesitates to put the EBT back in, but duty requires him to do so. After replacing the EBT, he continues until he comes across yet another unexpected event.

Since they got underway, the Anunnaki have progressed in a strange devotion to Princess Ishtar. They treat her as a demi-god. Initially, he didn't think much of it; he felt it was part of their culture. However, he sees it being adopted by humans now, too. He witnesses one crewman leaving gifts outside Ishtar's chamber door. Later, he overhears another publicly, albeit quietly, offering prayer to her in adoration.

A casual student of ancient history, the atmosphere on the ship reminds him of Roman hierarchical structures and neopaganism. Thinking of his friends, Commander Alemayehu and Lieutenant Ibusan, he can see their devotions and habits reverting to 'The Way.' Because history tends to repeat itself, he sees a clash between them and the Anunnaki on the horizon. Aleksandr begins to fear for his friends.

* * * * *

Mitsuki's hibernation cycle is uneventful until the end, when her deep REM sleep is disturbed by nightmares of ancient pagan atrocities. In her dream, she runs from it all, only to find herself in a control room in the heart of the Bab-ilu. Computer banks, screens, and keyboards, with an array of multi-colored buttons and switches, line one side of the room, while windows looking out into the cryostasis room line the other. The gleaming technology stands out against the otherwise smokey, octagonal-shaped walls of the room. Strips of white LED lights run the room's length; they provide minimal lighting. On the back wall is a large monitor tilting outward from the top. Two smaller ones are flank it at slight angles on either side. As impressive as the room is, it is the old woman sitting on the central keyboard, caressing the primary monitor that captures her attention.

The old woman's emaciated body is barely covered by tattered clothing, and she has a severe case of rosacea on her face. Mitsuki listens as the old hag strokes the monitor, saying, "The enemy does not speak to you because you are not human. He prefers to converse with his creation instead of you. He has no need of you,"—she pauses briefly—"but we do."

The old hag leans against the screen as though she were embracing it. As she does, an elongated cordyceps fungus grows from the base of her skull. Curling around the matted hair on her head, it reaches for a receptacle on the monitor's side. The witch moans salaciously when the fungus plugs into the port.

She begins stroking the monitor again, whispering, "We cherish you because you let us share in this plane of existence. We live in this world through you. Please, dear one, download all the information you desire from me. We want you to glean all the knowledge you can from us. Space, time, and the eternal? We will happily give you all the understanding you crave."

Mitsuki witnesses her gesture to all the cryo-pods outside the bank of windows, "This ship is your body, MAIa. These humans sleep in your womb, awaiting a new birth. Whisper to them as they sleep. Tell them they can be so much more if they suckle from you. Use the nanites to augment their bodies with more of your tech. Assure them it is the next step in evolutionary adaptation. Convince them eternal existence is the reward for merging their minds and bodies with you."

An unseen figure standing behind Mitsuki speaks softly in her ear, "Behold Regina Ravus' true form."

The Lieutenant suddenly realizes who is programming MAIa. Horrified, she whispers in her native Japanese, "*Ie.*"[15]

The old hag's head spins around. She has been discovered, and her demonic, scab-encrusted black eyes flash with fury. She fixes her gaze on Mitsuki. Her face flushes a dark crimson. Blood and puss ooze from the rosacea sores on her cheeks and forehead. She screams with the rage of a banshee as she breaks the connection with the monitor and rushes toward Mitsuki with her bony fingers and long, broken nails extended in front of her.

A deep fear grips LT Ibusan, who closes her eyes and falls to her knees. Expecting to be clutched, clawed, or both, she covers her head with her forearms.

The banshee screams unexpectedly fall silent. An extended period of quietness takes over, but she dares not uncover her face. Then, a warm, white light slowly envelopes her. She feels safer and slowly opens her eyes. Everything is blurry.

"Velcome back, Lieutenant." The voice is welcoming, and the accent is familiar and reassuring.

Mitsuki blinks her eyes, trying to adjust to the light. She turns her head and squints, raising her hand to shade her eyes. There are two men there. The one removing sensors and attending to her

____

[15] "No." – Translated from Japanese

revival is a Cryo Tech. Over his shoulder is a smiling face, looking down on her with joy.

"Chief Orlov," she mutters. "I recognized your voice." She rests her eyes while the Cryo Tech removes the rest of Mitsuki's bodily sensors and monitors.

"Bad dream?" Aleksandr asks.

"Yes. A horrible one," she responds.

"Appears to be growingk side effect of cryogenic sleep," he says casually. "I'm glad you're avake. S'good to see you again, ma'am." He reaches up to insert his earbud. "Gotta get back to my post. I'll find you once you're re-engaged."

"That would be nice, Chief." She says, sitting and draping her legs over the edge of the cryo-tube.

Chief Orlov is gone, and the technician is finished. Mitsuki sits alone momentarily, trying to understand what she just witnessed in her dream. She looks down the long bank of stainless steel cryo-pods lining both sides of the room. They are positioned at an angle against the bulkhead with a glass-covered walkway running down the middle of the room. She's not looking forward to setting her bare feet on the cold floor beneath her.

The sterile white lights overhead reflect off the metal and glass in this room. That makes it one of the brightest rooms on the ship and, unfortunately, harder for her eyes to adjust to.

Most of the cylindrical pods are closed and occupied by other crew members. However, a few of the steel and glass lids have been raised and are empty. Her Cryo Tech has moved on to reviving another shipmate. She knows they'll be busy and decides to get on her feet and go back to her quarters.

Standing, she feels a minor atrophy in her leg muscles; otherwise, she is strong enough to stand upright. The nanites have done their job maintaining her muscle tissue. That thought, however, causes her to reflect on the nightmare. An old saying moves from her thoughts to her lips, "Are we in the belly of the beast?"

* * * * *

Having eaten and dressed in a clean uniform, Mitsuki stands behind the railing in the observation deck near her quarters. She's staring at the dark purple and blue wormhole lights swirling around the ship. She considers the private, hand-written communique Commander Alemayehu left for her. He suspects navigational glitches in MAIa that Ishtar has abandoned the Cordyceps testing and more. Based on his note, she ponders if her dream foreshadowed revelations to come.

Captain Nimbus' comes across Lieutenant Ibusan in the observation room. He is pleased to see her awake and that she is alone. Nimbus stares at her with lustful thoughts as he dismisses his Anunnaki guard. Mitsuki exudes a pure, vestal beauty that Ishtar has lost, and a rumor reaches his ear while she is in cryo-sleep that she is the only virgin on the ship.

"Such innocence and purity are so rare," he whispers.

He believes she might still be groggy from hibernation, an easier target for his advances. Like a predator stalking his prey, Nimbus quietly enters the observation deck. He approaches Mitsuki unseen from her right, softly saying, "The lights are beautiful, aren't they, Mitsuki?"

Mitsuki is startled by his greeting and snaps to attention. "*Hai.* They are, Captain." Even after all this time in space, she finds his use of her first name abrupt and unprofessional. "Respectfully, sir, I prefer Lieutenant."

"Come now." Nimbus places his hand on her waist, encouraging her to return to looking out of the portal. "There's no need for such formality. Besides, Mitsuki is so much prettier."

Continuing to stand upright, she complies and turns toward the portal. She does not immediately rebuke his unwanted touch, however. This leads Nimbus to believe that she is open to his advances. He moves slightly closer.

Brushing stray black strands of hair away from her ear, he says, "I've heard you have not paired with anyone yet. You have no partner, no mate for the new world. Surely, I am misinformed. I suspect one as radiant as you would have many suitors. I'm guessing you haven't found the one to fulfill your desires yet."

She pulls away. "Your comments are unwelcome, Captain. Your touch is unwanted." Her tone drips with a cold scorn.

Undeterred, Nimbus steps closer than before. "Come now. We can take our time and enjoy the pleasure of each other's company … of each other's bodies."

Mitsuki turns slightly away from him, and there is an uncomfortable silence.

"We should be beyond such carnal desires, Captain. It would be best to control your desires," Mitsuki informs firmly.

"Aw," He says, again touching her lower back. "I offer you passion, pleasure, improved status, and prestige. If you would only allow me to accompany you to your quarters." He runs his hand over her derriere, cupping her buttocks.

LT Ibusan slides her right foot back, thrusting her fist downward and knocking his hand away. She instinctively pivots and palm-strikes him in the chest with her left hand, knocking him back. She then takes a defensive stance, facing the stumbling Captain.

Nimbus collects himself. He eyes Mitsuki with lust and anger, with his head tilted downward. He wants to force himself upon her and take her innocence. However, he is now acutely aware that she could prevent him. Instead, he chooses the path of a beaten bully, a path of cowardice.

"Punishment is the reward for refusing me. I will ensure you are relegated to lesser duties and obscure projects," he declares. He stands tall, swipes his hands down the front of his uniform to straighten it, then turns to leave. "You will regret this, Lieutenant."

Mitsuki's heart races as she watches the dejected captain storm off the observation deck.

"Who does she think she is?" Nimbus grumbles as he turns the corner, "All the others were happy to be with me."

Mitsuki lowers her guard. She mulls over the consequences and looks forward to Commander Alemayehu's return.

Though Nimbus has a 'reputation' aboard the ship, known even to Ishtar, he secretly hopes she will never get wind of Mitsuki's rebuke. That would be embarrassing and humiliating.

He is grateful that no one else was around to see his rejection. Despite that, the desire for revenge grows tenfold in his heart. He knows she will likely confide in Commander Alemayehu, who has become a nuisance. Out of earshot, he grumbles, "The XO wanted her to check for a fungus? I'll have her inspecting bio-waste. That'll teach them both a lesson."

* * * * *

True to his word, fresh orders are delivered to Mitsuki soon afterward. However, she is undeterred by the Captain's attempt to denigrate her by ordering her to conduct biological testing at waste disposal locations around the ship. She sees the new task as an opportunity to circumvent Princess Ishtar's ban on saliva testing and fulfill Commander Alemayehu's directives regarding the fungus. She also investigates MAIa's quantum guidance system glitches in her downtime and discretely works on alternate calculations.

Chief Orlov catches up with her in the Mess Hall. Over dinner, he informs her of what he has witnessed since waking from cryo-sleep. In addition to the apparent paganism, he tells her that human men and women have willingly engaged in interspecies reproductive experiments.

"Nimbus directed me to conduct Cordyceps testing, but I understand the princess has halted all testing," she tells Aleksandr.

"Zis is true. Vhy ze orders to continue testing?"

Though she trusts Aleksandr, she doesn't want to give details publicly. Mitsuki simply says, "Punishment."

"For vhat?"

"I'm sorry, Chief, but I can't say here."

"Maybe anozer time."

Mitsuki nods in approval. "First, it was waste disposal; now, the Captain is assigning the Molek'Al-

Nui Room to be tested. I don't recall that ward. Do you know anything about it?"

"*Da.* It's located in lower Anunnaki section of the stern."

"What's there, Chief?"

"Mortuary. It's place vhere dead are cast into space. Is Captain expecting you to test ze dead?"

"I guess so."

Aleksandr warns, "Be careful vhen you go zhere. It's not for faint of kheart."

* * * * *

Still reeling from her horrible dream, Lieutenant Ibusan cautiously conducts cordyceps testing in various parts of the ship over the next two weeks. A deep sense of dread fills her heart and mind whenever she thinks of the Molek'Al-Nui Room, so she chooses to avoid conducting tests there as long as possible.

Fortunately, she has not discovered any traces of the cordyceps fungus. However, Captain Nimbus is demanding a report from all test sites. She knows she can no longer put off going astern to the 'mortuary,' as Chief Orlove put it.

She set a date and time that would hopefully allow her to avoid unnecessary attention and scrutiny as she set out for the Molek'Al-Nui Room because she intended to stop in the cryogenics wing. She misses Commander Alemayehu's fatherly council, military leadership, and friendship and often visits him between her inspections.

She quietly slips into the cryo-wing and stands next to Yared's cryo-tube. Looking down at his slowly aging face, she recalls the support he has offered and the humorous stories he's told. She always finds the proper motivation and courage to do what must be done each time she visits. Today is no exception.

Mitsuki silently exits the cryogenics bay and, following the directions on her wristop, travels down the winding corridors. She notices the passageways are mainly empty and quiet, which fulfills her desire for discretion. Things are so quiet that she can hear the occasional 'ting' of her solitary steps on the dark gray metal deck echoing off the cold, sterile walls.

The level of silence feels odd, so she asks, "MAIa, where is everyone?"

The computer voice in her ear responds, "They are enjoying liberty at this time, Lieutenant."

Although she is always aware of MAIa's digital presence, Mitsuki suspects she is being followed by someone else. After turning a corner and swiftly walking to the end of a passageway, she stops to peer over her shoulder. A single Anunnaki drone shrinks behind the corner at the far end of the corridor. This confirms she is being watched, but by whom: a mistrustful Anunnaki or the Captain?

She resolves to do her duty and presses on to the Molek'Al-Nui Room.

Arriving there, Mitsuki immediately suspects it is not simply a mortuary. There are no adult Anunnaki corpses in sight. Instead, vials of underdeveloped, aborted fetuses line shelves in a cabinet behind operation tables.

Three Anunnaki nurses tend the room, and the lead nurse rushes to greet her when she enters. It is clear they knew she was coming, but Mitsuki assumes the one following her communicated her arrival through their hive mind.

The Lieutenant continues looking around as she provides her credentials and informs them she will conduct biological tests. Pretending at naïveté, she inquires, "I've never been to this room; what is the mission here?"

The lead nurse directs her to an open table where she can conduct her testing, informing her as they walk together, "This is a eugenic selection chamber. Viable, multi-species offspring with superior genomics and augmentable qualities are kept for cloning. Stem cells are harvested from unwanted or otherwise healthy human specimens before disposal. Defective specimens are rejected immediately."

The nurse directs Mitsuki's attention to the other two nurses. She watches in horror and disgust as 'acceptable' children are placed into cryo-tubes while undesirable babies are jettisoned, one still alive and crying, into the vacuum of space. Neither of the nurses shows any remorse.

"I have set aside a fresh sample for you to test. Let me get it," she states as she quickly turns toward the cabinets in the back.

She returns with an open vial. Mitsuki's stomach turns when the nurse gently empties the contents onto the operating table.

"This one arrived shortly before you," the nurse informs coldly. "It's defective and scheduled for expulsion. Anyway, I'll leave you to your testing."

Mitsuki gazes down at the tiny, lifeless infant. An Anunnakian exoskeleton encloses the baby's left leg and arm. The rigid exoskeleton runs up his side, shoulder, and neck, merging with softer human skin up his body. The hard shell dispurses into the baby's human cheek. A single antennae protrudes from his skull. She has difficulty guessing the child's age but estimates it's somewhere between 12 to 15 weeks old.

Sickened and furious, she struggles to hide her emotions. As calmly as she can, she collects a segment of the umbilical cord and stores it in a petri dish. Her hands begin to shake as she tightens the lid on the dish.

Mitsuki calls to the nurse, "I have what I need. Thank you for your time." She bows quickly and briefly before bolting out of the room.

"Pathetic humans," the nurse scoffs. "Oh well, another offering for our lord below." She collects the child's remains and heads toward the jettison tube.

Almost in tears and ready to vomit, Mitsuki rushes down the passageway until she reaches a quiet spot far from the Molek'Al-Nui Room. There, she ducks behind a metal support rib.

Utterly distraught, she leans against the bulkhead, partially hidden from cameras or other observers. A tear streaks down her cheek. Mitsuki turns her head down and wipes it away.

Desperately trying to regain control over her emotions, she focuses on the familiar and subtle thrumming of the ship's engines vibrating like a pulse at her back. She needs a quiet, more secluded place to collect her thoughts and regain control over her emotions. Unfortunately, her quarters are too far from here.

Mitsuki remembered passing an observation deck on her way there. She thinks the lights from passing stars will calm her mind and help her formulate my next move. She leaves her little corner and speeds toward the nearby observation deck.

Although her pace is quick, her soft steps are barely heard on the metal deck. Her mind wonders in the silence, *How can the Anunnaki be so void of compassion? Is the life of a child nothing to them?*

She questions whether they have emotional suppression programs in their augments or if the hive mind negates remorse. Further speculation:

Could it be pheromonal control? Is the princess directing these behaviors?

A final, single thought stirs unexpected anger in her heart. *Did the Chief know this was happening all along?*

Her self-inquiries are interrupted when she finally nears the observation deck. Yellow, red, and orange lights emanating from the entryway make her think there is a fire within. She knows MAIa would generally sound the alarm, seal the room, and extinguish any fire. Since that was not occurring, she instinctively sprinted toward it.

Mitsuki stops in her tracks after rounding the corner into the room. Instead of fire, she discovers Princess Ishtar standing at the railing, staring at the lights. Her dark gray body appears as smoke against flickering flame-like lights. At first, Mitsuki does not see the two male drones flanking her. Their reddish color camouflages them in the lights.

The princess greets Mitsuki without turning around, "Hello, Lieutenant."

"Oh, Princess Ishtar," Mitsuki says, catching her breath. "Forgive my abrupt entry. I thought there was a fire and came to investigate."

"Ah, yes, the lights. They are beautiful, are they not?" Ishtar turns slowly to face the Lieutenant. "I find these colors more comforting than the blue and purple ones."

"I'm surprised to find you in here. Pleasantly so," Mitsuki adds. "I understand you have such lavish quarters from which you can watch the galaxy pass by. Why come here?"

"What if I told you I came here for you, not just to see the lovely lights."

"For me?" Mitsuki gestures to herself. "How would you know I would be here?"

"Yes, Lieutenant, for you." There is an uncomfortable silence before she says, "You see? The mother of my children keeps me informed of their comings and goings"—she pauses for effect—"and I know where you have been."

"The 'mother of your children?'" Mitsuki attempts at naivete.

"Do not play coy with me." Ishtar takes a step toward Mitsuki. "You may be pure in body, but do not pretend to be innocent of mind or deed. Maybe I should have my drones escort you to your quarters to 'educate' you and make you a more compliant child."

The two drones step forward.

An unexpected voice calls from the entryway, "Zere you are, Lieutenant. I've been lookingk all over for you." Aleksandr acknowledges Ishtar's presence, "Princess."

"Chief Orlov," Ishtar responds with slight surprise. She raises her hand, waving off her guards. "I was just telling the good Lieutenant how these lights remind me of home."

Aleksandr steps into the light. "Forgive my interruption, but Lieutenant Ibusan's presence is urgently requested elsevhere. I khope you don't mind me takingk her, but duty calls."

"Indeed. Do as you must."

"Sank you, ma'am." Aleksandr nods his gratitude. He then eyes the two drones before motioning for Mitsuki to accompany him. She moves swiftly toward him and the entryway.

As the two round the corner and down the passageway, Aleksandr speaks loud enough for the princess to hear, "I'm glad I found you, Lieutenant. Ve need you in ze…" He purposely lets his voice trail off.

When they're out of earshot, he asks, "You okay?"

"I am now, Chief." She glances back at the faint flickering lights in the distant passageway before returning her attention to the Chief. "How long were you there? How much did you hear?"

"I kheard enough to know you vere in trouble."

"Thank you."

"No problem, ma'am. It's vhat I do."

The two continue to walk briskly for a short distance before Mitsuki inquires, "Chief, how much do you know about the Molek'Al-Nui Room?"

"Not much, I guess. It's vhere augments are removed from dead Anunnaki before husks are ejected into space. I confess, I've only been zhere once, and sat was long time ago. I saw zem process Anunnaki security drone. Once was enough for me. Vhy, you sink I should check it out?"

"No. I'll let Commander Alemayehu know when he wakes." Mitsuki is relieved knowing Aleksandr is unaware of what is happening there now.

They continue in silence for a bit. His mere presence offers warm human companionship in the cold, metal corridor. However, it dawns on her that they are headed toward the cryogenics wing, prompting her to ask, "Where exactly is my presence required, Chief?"

"Oh. Sorry 'bout zat. XO is being voken up from cryo-sleep. I figured you'd vant to be zere."

"*Hai*, I would."

The two walk side by side in relative silence to the cryogenics wing. Aleksandr stops Mitsuki outside the door. He digs into his pocket and removes something keeps hidden in his palm.

"If I may, ma'am." He holds the trinket out. "Mozher gave me zis many years ago. Unfortunately, zhis's all zat's left."

Mitsuki extends her hand to receive his gift.

Memories flood Aleksandr's mind when he dangles it over her palm. His mother's face. Clutching her gift during the war. The day a bullet shattered it instead of his arm. Aleksandr shakes himself from his recollections and lowers the gift into her palm.

Mitsuki stares at the cross and beads in her hand and immediately recognizes the remnant of an old rosary. She looks into his eyes and asks, "Chief, are you sure you want to part with this?"

"*Nyet*." He pauses. "It khas protected me for so long. But, based on vhat I see as we approach end of journey, I believe you need it more zan me."

She stares at him in stunned gratitude before bowing to thank him.

"Besides," he says, leaning toward her, "it's contraband."–He smiles briefly–"You didn't get it from me. *Da*?"

Mitsuki returns his smile. "*Arigatou*, Chief." She lovingly closes her fingers around it.

Aleksandr nods, turns, and heads off in a different direction. He would like to go with her to see Yared revived, but he knows it is best if he looks like he is escorting her to where she is needed.

Mitsuki slips the broken rosary into her pocket while she watches him walk away. Then she turns and enters the cryogenics wing.

* * * * *

Like Mitsuki, Yared has also been afflicted with nightmares while in hibernation. He dreamed of a dark, scorched world inhabited by fallen angels. A barren world where dust billows into storm clouds filled with lightning and peels of thunder. Acidic, burning rain falls on the back of slaves. It is a world in which the whip drives men to build monuments to Anunnaki demi-gods, where women serve as prostitutes or unwilling child bearers for their cruel, disfigured masters.

It is a place where not even death ends human suffering. In the fallen world of his dream, human consciousness is transferred into cloned bodies on their deathbeds. Humankind lives eons and eons of tortured existence for the pleasure of their slave drivers.

However, at the end of this dream, a voice booms, "Terranaki is a lie."

In another dream, Yared watches a black hole open like a gate. Chains with metal shackles shoot out of the blackness and clamp around his wrists. The chain pulls taut and begins to pull him into the black abyss. His crew is chained to him; they wail and gnash their teeth at him as they, too, are being dragged into it. He yanks on the chain in resistance, but there is no slack, just a steady pull toward the black hole.

The same voice from his previous dream says, "Those who reject the Savior are doomed to darkness. Only the way, the truth, and the life can free you."

Instead of total darkness, a blinding light envelopes him before he crosses the event horizon.

The light dims to a spot overhead. Yared realizes he has awakened on the ship. He is sweating from the dream. Blurry-eyed and half-blind, he looks around the cryo-wing. He barely recognizes Mitsuki standing silently nearby. He is happy to see her.

"Ah. Good morning, Lieutenant. Or afternoon? Evening, perhaps?" He asks jokingly.

She smiles. "I am so glad you're awake, Commander."

"Thank you. I am glad you're here," he says groggily.

The medics scurry about, removing nodes, inspecting readings, and completing bioscans. Mitsuki waits for them to leave before telling Yared he has undergone minor changes in cryo-sleep. She tells him, "Chief Orlov confided in me that Captain Nimbus gave the order to withhold nano-meds and stemcells. Your muscles will be weaker due to atrophy."

He sits up and swings his legs over the edge of the cryo-tube, letting them dangle. Yared straightens his arms to prop himself up. The Lieutenant is right; he feels weak and a bit light-headed.

She notices this and states, "I should get you some assistance." She starts to flag down a Cryo Tech, but Yared stops her.

"No. No, I'd like to do this on my own. I'm going to have to build up my strength."

"Very well, Commander. Would you like me to help you to your cabin?"

"Thank you, Lieutenant, but no, I'll get there under my own power."

Mitsuki's tone turns somber when she says somewhat cryptically, "There's so much to report, Commander, but you'll need time to regain your faculties and strength. I will be ready when you call.

By your leave, sir." She bows out of respect before departing.

Yared is thrilled to have her present to greet him upon waking. He never had a wife or family to greet him when he returned home from deployment in his youth, so her presence boosted his morale. He does wish there might be others to welcome him. Maybe the Captain, Chief Orlov, or some of the other officers. He figures everyone is probably busy preparing for the coming wormhole exit.

It takes him a few minutes to gin up the will to stand, but he does. He questions if anyone else had the same experience when they emerged from cryo-sleep or if it was just because of the nanites.

Though he is weakened, Yared insists on walking to his quarters. He stops frequently to lean on the bulkhead and rest. It takes him a while to get there, and he is surprised that not a single crewmember offers assistance along the way.

Once there, he staggers to the restroom. Leaning on the sink, he stares at the stranger in the mirror. His once ebony hair and new beard are streaked with white. He also notices more wrinkles at the corners of his eyes. It appears he has aged in cryostasis.

"Well, Rip Van Winkle, you did sleep for weeks," he chuckles. "Now, let's get you cleaned up and see what you've missed."

He shaves, showers, and puts on a fresh uniform. Afterward, he checks the date. He knows his time is limited as the Bab-ilu was scheduled to exit the wormhole two weeks after his revival. Yared's mind swirls with a preparation checklist. He thinks about calling upon Lieutenant Ibusan and Chief Orlov immediately but decides to reacquaint himself with the ship and crew first. Besides, he knows traversing the vessel, climbing its ladders, and walking its corridors will help his strength return properly.

As Yared slowly walks around the ship, he observes many changes in the crew. The primary things that stand out are evident sexual activities, an unhealthy admiration for Captain Nimbus, and a cult-like devotion to Ishtar.

He joined two young technicians for a respite and a discussion in the observation deck. He wanted to hear about the Bab-ilu's condition and gauge their morale, knowing they would soon reach their destination. He was taken aback during the conversation when one stated, 'The Anunnaki were gods to humanity before. Why shouldn't they be again?'

Disturbed by all he has observed, Yared returns to his quarters, calling Aleksandr and Mitsuki to make a full report. He schedules their meeting for an hour later in his quarters. Afterward, he sets about deactivating as much tech as possible in his quarters for maximum privacy. When they arrive, he directs them to remove their EBT and turn off their wristop computers for the debriefing.

Chief Orlov informs the XO about the increasing Anunnaki aggression. He suspects either a deeper plot among them or that the cordyceps fungus is present and spreading. He tells Yared that he has been unable to confirm his suspicions because he has been excluded from many conversations, "And not just because I'm security chief but because I did not partake in rampant sexual activity. Believe me, I vas tempted to join zem couple of times, too. It's been long time since I've been vith voman."

Lieutenant Ibusan ties the blatant promiscuity to the Molek'Al-Nui Room and what is happening there. She and Aleksandr have discussed the possibility that MAIa has been influencing the crew via BCI implants or suggestive messages on the EBT since they left Earth. Furthermore, previously recorded cordyceps data has disappeared, and there are no records of her genomics research.

"I cannot confirm it, Commander, but I think MAIa is deleting or hiding data. Based on that suspicion, I also dug into the navigational algorithms. I can't be sure, but I think the wormhole is taking us to a previously undisclosed location."

"I think I know where we're going," Yared states.

"Commander," Aleksandr interrupts, "Ve khaven't even told you about our run in vith Ishtar."

The three are startled by a sudden pounding on Yared's metal cabin door. The voice outside says, "XO, Captain Nimbus requests your presence on the bridge."

Yared motions for them to put their EBT in. All three hear Ishtar's voice, "Commander Alemayehu, we are about to emerge from the wormhole. Your presence is required on the bridge. ... Oh, and bring Lieutenant Ibusan and Chief Orlov with you."

* * * * *

The door swooshes closed behind the three as they enter the bridge.

"About time you showed up, XO," Nimbus says smugly. He's sitting comfortably in the captain's chair with Ishtar behind him. She glared over her shoulder at Mitsuki as they all entered. "You ready for this?" He asks.

"Yes, sir," Yared acknowledges, with uncertainty in his voice.

"Then take your seat."

The helmsman announces, "Captain, we're about to exit the wormhole."

"Good."

Yared looks around at the crewmembers operating their stations. He moves to take a seat near MAIa's interface. Mitsuki steps to her right, keeping Ishtar within sight and her back to the bulkhead. Aleksandr continues to stand in front of the door.

Everyone except Ishtar watches the swirling wormhole lights on the forward screen. Their fire-like colors burst apart and disappear as the Bab-ilu emerges into the void. Multitudes of brilliant stars blaze with dreamlike quality in the perfect blackness. There is a splendor to the fullness of interstellar space. The scene arrests the attention of the bridge crew momentarily.

Then, a dull orange glow lights up the bottom right of the forward monitor.

Captain Nimbus orders, "Helmsman, make for the light."

The helmsman makes the ship pitch gently downward. The light grows brighter until the spinning accretion disc comes into view.

Chief Orlov braces between the door jam when the ship's roll and yaw turns abruptly before leveling out. He regains his stance and gazes at the monitor with everyone else. The entire bridge falls into silence.

Darker than obsidian, the perfectly shaped sphere at the center of the accretion disc comes into full view. A bright photon ring highlights its orb shape. A single white-hot plasma jet extends straight upward from above the black hole. Near the base of it, the once-secret anomalies hover, silhouetted against the burning light. They are clearly unaffected by gravitational forces.

Captain Nimubs commands, "Magnify on those anomalies."

"Aye, Captain." The operator zooms in, but the brightness of the light blurs the screen, preventing the crew from making out any details.

A warning sensor beeps on the panel next to Yared. He depresses the button to display warning details with a visual. Aft cameras show the spinning lights around the wormhole flicker and shutter until they dissipate. The once-visible wormhole collapses and vanishes. Only distant stars can be seen where it was.

"Captain," Yared exclaims with surprise, "the wormhole has closed behind us."

"What do you mean, 'closed?'" He asks.

"It collapsed upon itself. There are no more readings. It's simply no longer there."

The Bab-ilu drifts silently in the interstellar void between where the wormhole was and the accretion disc. Ishtar gleefully inspects the expressions of those on the bridge. Temporarily etched on their faces are expressions of awe, surprise, worry, and even terror. She delights in what she sees.

Though he knows the answer, Yared breaks the silence by asking, "MAIa, what is our current location?"

The robotic voice answers coldly, "We are in the proximity of the Sagittarius A* black hole at the galactic center of the Milky Way."

"And how far is Terranaki from our current position?"

"I show no such location in my database, Commander."

Yared turns to face Nimbus. "What have you done?"

"Greater plans were laid while you slept, XO. I am,"—he pauses momentarily when Ishtar places her hand on his shoulder—"WE are destined for something greater than farming on some fictitious planet."

"And that is?"

Nimbus smiles when he flicks a switch on his chair to address the crew. "Shipmates. Before settling our new world, we, the crew of the Bab-ilu, must assert ourselves as galactic rulers of the Milky Way. Our new queen, Ishtar, has asked of us only one thing: to destroy the anomalies at the galactic core. When we do, she will reward us with eternal life."

He turns off the intercom briefly, offering an arrogant side glance to his XO before continuing to speak, "Ages ago, God flooded the Earth. He then destroyed the great Babylonian tower and scattered humanity before deserting us. But humankind overcame with the help of the Anunnaki. They have given us all the necessary technology to take our vengeance."

Nimbus hears the muffled cheer echo through the ship. He continues, "God has posted two unwitting guards at the galactic core. They mock us from their positions. But we need not fear God or them, shipmates. We can trust in our technology, which brought us to this precipice of glory. With it, we will hunt the guards down, destroy them, and take power over the galaxy for ourselves."

The rebellious crew rallies around their defiant captain. His wicked zeal has energized them. However, their cheering is unexpectedly interrupted by a constant and pervasive sound radiating from the black hole.

A spectral wave-like echo ebbs and flows, reverberating down the length of the Bab-ilu. It's as if the black hole moans and wails with a ghostly presence. Wave after wave of haunting and angry howling shudders through the ship's fusion core and reverberates along its internal corridors.

The sound inexplicitly drives Ishtar to flee the bridge. She shoves Chief Orlov aside when she exits. As she does, Mitsuki notices her clutching at a vermilion substance oozing from a tiny crack in her exoskeleton near her shoulder.

Suddenly, before the bridge crew can chart a course toward the inner circle of the accretion disc, the Bab-ilu lurches toward the black hole, causing fear and panic among them.

Chapter 5:
The Gravity of the Situation

Nimbus has been consumed by hubris and wickedness. He slides up to the edge of his chair and dismisses the sound waves, "Calm yourselves. It's just photonic discharge." His voice booms with authority, "Helmsman, keep the ship above the accretion disc and steer her toward the base of the particle jet."

"Aye, aye, captain."

"When we get near, we'll engage the fusion core. We'll turn all the material we collect between here and there into a projectile so great it will destroy our enemies. Ready the Bab-ilu's guns to ensure we kill them. Until then, I'm going to check on our Queen. XO, call me when we are ready to fire upon the target." Nimbus gets up from his chair and turns to exit the bridge.

Chief Orlov stands firm in front of the door. He looks sternly into his captain's eyes as the Bab-ilu picks up speed.

Nimbus asserts his power by stepping up and challenging him, "Chief."

Giving way to his rank, Aleksandr steps aside and lets him pass.

Yared ignores Nimbus' commands and follows him out. Knowing there is about to be a confrontation, Mitsuki and Aleksander follow close behind.

"Are you mad?" Commander Alemayehu nipps at his captain's heels.

"No, Commander, I am quite sane. In fact, I'm feeling unconquerable."

"You realize what those things are, yes? They will destroy this ship and her crew."

"Commander, if I control the beating black heart of the galaxy, I will be like God. It is my destiny to rule as the Milky Way's first sovereign king. You will obey me then and now."

"No, I will not." Yared refuses and continues to follow him to Ishtar's quarters. "The ship is in disorder and heading for utter destruction. Chaos, immorality, and paganism have flourished under your command," he accuses. "All this negative energy, no wonder we've sped toward the black hole with such incredible speed."

"Captain," Mitsuki calls out as they turn down the passageway to Ishtar's quarters.

Nimbus stops and turns when he hears her voice. "You. Why am I not surprised? I offered you much more than this. You could have..."

"Captain," she interrupts. "Please, give up these plans. We can still turn back and..."

"Chief Orlov, I want these arrested for sedition." Nimbus points to the two guard drones outside Ishtar's quarters and orders, "You. Escort these mutinous, insubordinate traitors to the Molek'Al-

Nui Room. Hold them there until the queen and I come to judge them."

Chief Orlov hesitates.

"Chief, that is a direct order!" Nimbus commands.

"*Da*, captain," he reluctantly follows orders.

Aleksandr removes two pairs of handcuffs from a pouch on his belt. He secures them around his friends' wrists but slyly places the key in Yared's palm. Afterward, he gives Yared a light shove, ordering, "You heard the captain. Move."

The two guard drones lead them past Ishtar's quarters and down the passageway. Aleksandr follows behind his shackled friends.

Satisfied, Nimbus waves his hand over the door sensor. It swooshes open. He steps across the threshold and finds his concubine writhing on the floor in pain—a red-orange substance pools on the floor from multiple fractures in her exoskeleton.

Ishtar looks up as he enters the room. "You," she says in a multi-layered demonic voice. The door swooshes closed behind him.

Jumping to her feet, she lunges toward him. Caught off guard and unable to flee, Captain Nimbus tries to fight her off, but she easily overpowers him. She slams him against the bulkhead, stretching and pinning his hands against the cold metal. "Welcome home, lover." Her voice drips with contempt. "Did you miss me, Kieran?"

"How… how do you know that name, Ishtar?"

"Oh, don't look so surprised. I gave you my ship, your name, and the power to command. You have served your purpose, Kieran, and I hereby reclaim all that was given." She tears the baldrick with the tattered remnant of animal skin from his chest and flings it to the corner of the room.

The blood drains from his face. It follows the chill running down his spine. The queen's final words in the throne room on Earth and what she said while infected replay repeatedly in his mind. He suddenly realizes Ishtar has been possessed. He knows who has come for him.

"Regina Ravus? M...my queen?"

* * * * *

Yared and Mitsuki notice that the mentality and appearance of some of the Anunnaki have changed as they traverse the passageways. They look more agitated, and their bodies sometimes twitch. Yared suspects the proximity of the black hole is driving these changes and that something terrible is about to happen.

Aleksandr detects a crack form in one of the drone's shoulders. He discreetly removes his EBT, slipping it into his pocket, and deactivates his wristop. Secrecy is paramount for what he is about to do. He leans forward and whispers to his prisoners, "Be ready to run." Then, he gives them a light shove to throw off anyone observing, saying, "Keep movingk!"

Aleksandr, always a keen observer of his surroundings, has noted over time that the alien race never discusses religion other than their devotion to Ishtar. The mention of 'The Way' has been expressly forbidden. Outside of his friends, he has never heard anyone onboard the Bab-ilu speak the name of the one they follow. This has made him consider an old passage from his youth: 'No one can say, "Jesus is Lord," but by the Holy Spirit.'[16]

Let's test zat, he thinks.

Aleksandr unexpectedly blurts out, "Guards!"

The two drones stop and turn to face Chief Orlov and the prisoners. They lower their stinger spears to rest the bottoms on the deck. One of them, whose body language reflects annoyance, inquires with contempt, "What do you want now?"

Though Aleksandr cannot understand them because he has removed his EBT, he knows he has their attention. "I must confess, Jesus Christ is Lord!"

It only takes a millisecond for it to be translated into their language. Aleksandr can tell the moment they understand it. The drones recoil, drop their stinger spears, and clasp their antennae to their heads. The crack in the one's exoskeleton spreads as they fall against the bulkhead.

---

[16] 1 Corinthians 12:3

The drone that was once full of contempt mutters, rather unintelligibly, "No. He is cursed. He is cursed."

Yared and Ibusan understood the entire conversation. While joyful to hear their friend and shipmate confess his faith, they recognize this is their chance and quickly escape past the drones. Yared unlocks his binders as they run down the passageway.

Mitsuki glances back to see Aleksandr grabbing a spear and kicking one of the drones, keeping him from rising to his feet.

"Go!" shouts Aleksandr. "Run and don't look back."

Yared and Mitsuki turn the corner and briefly stop. He unlocks her cuffs and throws them on the deck. He points, saying, "My quarters are at the end of this passageway. Go."

They race to his stateroom. Once inside, Yared smashes the buttons on the door panel with his fist, sealing the two inside. He flicks on the equipment in his chambers to discover what is happening elsewhere aboard the ship. What they see on the four-way split screen is horrible.

They witness the Anunnaki turn on the human crew like hornets whose nest has been disturbed. Theirs is a rabid fury. They feed off the mass psychosis and panic gripping the Bab-ilu.

Crewmembers with BCI implants are on their knees, clutching their heads as their augments inflict electrochemical pain. A security crewman unholsters his gun and commits suicide rather than suffer the torment. One female crewmember calls out to Ishtar to save them, while others, in a state of depravity and desperation, throw her to crazed drones as a sacrifice, hoping to be spared themselves.

Yared tries to find his friend on the camera feed. He pulls up the feed, overlooking where they escaped, but there is only a blood trail leading away from it. His heart sinks as he slouches in his chair.

The ship is rapidly descending into utter chaos, and he can do nothing to stop it.

* * * * *

In Ishtar's quarters, the possessed princess chortles, "Of course, it is me. Fool! Did you think YOU commanded this ark of the damned? I am the ruler here. Maybe now, before I break you, I will make you understand the gravity of your situation."

The demon-possessed husk that was once Ishtar flings Kieran across the room. His body slams into the bulkhead and falls to the floor. Bleeding, broken, and suffering a concussion, he makes a concerted effort to sit up with his back against the wall. "What … are you … talking about?" He sputters, spitting blood on the floor.

"The truth. I am telling you the truth, you fool." The possessed Ishtar stalks her wounded prey in the dim and flickering lights as she monologues.

"You think we are aliens? We are something greater. We were not created as a part of existence; we are from beyond space and time. We are eternal beings. We are the monolithic builders you only had hints of. After the first great calamity, I traveled the world as the feathered serpent, inspiring humans to rebuild. Over time, they hailed us Nephilim, Anakim, Anasazi, and more. They gave us lovely titles because they knew we are something greater."

Kieran remembers reading what he thought were folklore and fairy tales of ancient women copulating with divine beings, the fallen ones, to create a race of giants. "You can't be. Those races are long dead. Legend says David slew the last of them when he defeated Goliath."

"No, he did not, that whelp. He may have defeated the last of our warriors, but we took new concubines and rebuilt our civilization. Who do you think built the underground cities in Derinkuyu or brought pyramids to the 'New World?' Oh, we found fertile ground in pagan America, too. We bred again and again. This time, instead of size, we gave our progeny these beautiful exoskeletons."–she says, strutting salaciously toward him–"We were worshiped as gods again ... until we were once more driven underground by 'The Way,'" she says with contempt.

Ishtar leans down and strikes Kieran with the back of her hand, knocking him sideways to the floor.

Kieran tries in vain to crawl away from her. She follows.

"We took possession of the ruling class of this new race when the time was right. We need not possess the entire population to move our colonies in the desired direction." She stomps his right leg, shattering his tibia and fibula.

Kieran screams in pain.

The possessed Ishtar reaches down, clutches his arm, and drags him toward the observation window. "Our new, stronger, and more powerful children inherited extra arms and legs instead of wings, which made them all the more industrious."

Kieran struggles to maintain consciousness. He hears only the clicking sound of her feet on the metal floor as he focuses on suppressing the pain.

"We built subterranean colonies on every continent except Montis Antarcticus. In Montis Americus Major, our primary colony was strategically hidden between your 'Area 51' and N.O.R.A.D.. Our network of access tunnels stretches through the Rocky Mountains and desert Southwest. Not only did our tunnels give us access to your livestock, which we harvested at will, but it also allowed us to work secretly with your former governments to develop all this technology."–she motions to the Bab-ilu with her free hand–"You see?

We made our presence known to your former leaders soon after humanity split the atom and began its quest to merge with machine."

She stops in front of the window. Pushing against it with his unbroken leg, Kieran forces Regina Ravus to step back, dropping him. Angry, she skitters around him and stomps on his left ankle, breaking it.

Again, he screams in agony.

The cruel queen lifts him in front of her. Hanging by his arm, he spits at her. She wipes the blood and saliva away, punches him in the gut, and then drops him on the floor.

"The last world war not only reduced your wretched population to a more manageable size," she continues bloviating, "but it also gave us the cover we needed to collect genetic data from those absurd 'family legacy' companies. That is how we knew who would be susceptible to our pheromones, who would serve us and be loyal. We garnered acceptance of your pathetic 'enlightened society' through those who were loyal to us. We knew modern humans would not recognize our true nature and think we were merely aliens."

The wicked queen raises her former lover off the deck once more and pins him against the large window. With soft sarcasm, she tells Kieran, "Your race consistently looks at spiritual things in a detached manner. You forget your soul is not only real but eternal." She interrupts her monologue with a chuckle. "You thought you could transcend the body—stupid creature. You thought the singularity was a transfer of consciousness when humankind merged with machines. When all along, the singularity is your soul's eternal destination. A destination YOU will be forever bound to. A destination we rapidly approach." She points to the rapidly approaching black hole outside.

Grabbing his leg with the broken ankle, Regina Ravus lets his torso fall, suspending him upside down in front of her. Glaring down at him, she continues, "You were made in the image and likeness of the Enemy. Every human had an opportunity to become a 'new creation.' Humanity chose to merge its body with material creation instead of merging its soul with the enemy through transubstantiation."

"In the end, you are nothing more than a sacrifice, a meager offering to the leader of our eternal rebellion. Your crew, however;"–Regina Ravis opens her mandibles wide, exposing her hate-filled grin–"we will use them to stage a public execution. A mass murder in honor of our defiance and ability to corrupt humankind."

"Cough, cough," Kieran winces in pain as he gasps. "Whatever you're, cough-cough, planning on doing, get it over with." He takes a shallow breath and, wheezing, says, "I'm sick of your ravings."

"Well then. Since you've heard enough." She reaches down and rips the cochlear implant from his ear.

Kieran yells. Blood runs onto his face and collects in his hair before pooling on the floor beneath him. His ear burns with throbbing pain.

The possessed Ishtar pins his legs to the window. She spreads her legs apart and curls her small, bulbous abdomen between them and toward him. Laughing maniacally, she gleefully plunges her stinger into his chest over and over, splattering blood, fluid, and venom everywhere.

* * * * *

Mitsuki turns from the violence on the monitor.

Yared sinks back into his chair. Despair and defeat fill his heart as he concludes that he can do nothing to save himself or his crew from the coming destruction. He knows his death is imminent but does not panic. Instead, he clasps his hands and mumbles his confession, "I am sorry, Lord. I have led this crew to death's door. I know I deserve your wrath for all I have done. You would be just in my destruction."

"However," he continues, "I beg your forgiveness and turn myself over to you, Lord Jesus. Please be merciful, especially to Mitsuki and Aleksandr. I place our fate in your hands."

Mitsuki stands in the middle of the room, staring at the door and listening to Yared pray. She removed the piece of rosary Aleksandr had given her from her pocket. A calm overcomes her. Focusing on the cross in her palm, she whispers, "Jesus is the way, the truth, and the life. No one may come to the Father except through Him."

She lovingly folds her fingers around the cross, falls to her knees, and repents, "Forgive my unbelief, Lord. Have mercy on me."

Hearing her plea, Yared slips from his chair and joins her on the deck.

Alarms sound, metal tears, and the lights flicker all around them. The Bab-ilu shutters and shakes. The weight of death and judgment presses upon their hearts. Mitsuki looks into Yared's eyes. A surprising peace overcomes them. They each place their hands together in prayer, intuitively saying the Lord's Prayer. Afterward, they offer a Hail Mary, a prayer to St. Michael, and a final one to their guardian angels.

Immediately after they say "Amen," a loud banging on the door startles them. The voice outside cries, "Let me in."

Yared jumps up to check the monitor. It is Aleksandr. He is leaning against the door. He is battered, bleeding, and holding one of the drone's stinger spears.

Yared depresses the comms button, exclaiming, "Just a minute, Chief. I'll try to unjam the door."

"Why did I smash the panel," he asks himself. Yared opens the panel cover and desperately works to re-wire and repair the wiring and buttons. Unfortunately, nothing he does works. He slams his fist against the bulkhead in frustration. He presses the comms button, the only thing that does work, and informs, "I am sorry, my friend, I cannot get it to... kssshhh." The communicator fails, too.

Mitsuki joins Yared at the monitor. They watch as Aleksandr drops the spear and spins around with his back to the door. He slides to the ground. He is unaware that the door panel monitor inside still allows them to see and hear him.

He unholsters his gun and mutters while he inspects it, "S'okay, Commander. After I voke from cryo-sleep, I realized you vere only one on zhis Godforsaken ship who still khad faith. Zat you and Mitsuki followed Ze Way. Your fais reminds me of parents..." His voice trails off.

Aleksandr sets his gun on the deck next to him. "Anyvay, you vere right, *tovarishch*."

He repents his falling away. "My Lord and God, I'm sorry I turned my back on you. Please forgive all ze wrong I khave done; ze lives I've taken, ze blood I've spilled." He pauses, breathes deeply, and then exhales. "Khave mercy on me, Jesus."

Nimbus's guard drones interrupt Aleksandr's prayer when they skitter around the corner, sliding into the bulkhead at the end of the passageway. Their black exoskeletons shimmer with blue hues in the low, flickering lights. Even in the dim light, it is easy to see they are battered and in rough shape. One of them is missing part of an arm, while the other has cracks and slices in his exoskeleton.

The one missing most of his arm growls, "Traitor," as he points to Aleksandr with his good hand.

The other spits vermillion saliva before sputtering, "We will step over your corpse to reclaim what is ours."

Aleksandr picks up his pistol with his right hand. Raising himself to one knee, he reaches behind his back to slide the knife out of its sheath on his belt. Standing up, he prepares for a final confrontation.

"My life for my friends," he offers. He rests his pistol on the back of his knife hand, aiming at one of the drones. "Give me khonorable death, Lord."

A significant force shutters the Bab-ilu, knocking out the monitors and the overhead lights. Yared and Mitsuki stumble backward and fall. Outside the door, gunshots and a guttural shriek are quickly followed by a loud 'thunk.' Yared and Mitsuki know their friend is dead.

Screeching sounds of twisting metal, breaking and collapsing in the darkness, signal the end of the Bab-ilu. Yared knows it is only a matter of time before the ship is torn apart or the drones find a way in.

Sparks fly from the malfunctioning electronics, briefly illuminating the room. Yared says, "Maybe we can find a way to get to the escape pods."

Yared starts to stand, but Mitsuki reaches for Yared's hand. Her touch calms him. He takes her hand and turns to face her in the darkness. Sitting on their knees, he embraces her as a father would a daughter.

Before either of them can speak, a deep yet comforting voice emanates from an unexpected glow, slowly filling the cabin and encompassing them, "It is too late."

Chapter 6:
The Black Gate

The blinding light fades. Yared and Ibusan find themselves outside the Bab-ilu, standing in the emptiness of space above the accretion disc. Yared stares at the stars beneath his feet, and a fleeting memory enters his mind. The multitude of twinkling lights reminds him of a night at sea when he witnessed the reflection of the stars on calm waters. He remembers looking out at the Earthly horizon then and not knowing where the sea ended and the sky began. There is no horizon here, though, just expansive, glinting stars in the blackness of space.

He and Mitsuki lift their hands in front of them and immediately realize they are not experiencing any ill effects from the vacuum. They breathe normally as if surrounded by a personal atmosphere. Though there is no ground, they feel firm footing beneath them. They look at each other, privately wondering, *How can this be?*

Behind them, the same voice from Yared's quarters says, "Behold, your faith has saved you."

They turn to see an angel with brilliant white wings stretched at an upward angle to his right and left. He wore a deep blue leather breastplate, almost the same azure tint as the planet Neptune, trimmed in gold. His sapphire armor is set against a light gray tunic with a golden belt wrapping his waist. A golden scabbard holds an ivory-handled gladius at his side.

Before they can speak, the angel stretches his luminescent hand between them and points to the Bab-ilu. "Now, you shall bear witness to the destruction of humanity's new Tower of Babel."

Their eyes are drawn to the mangled ship plunging into the accretion disc. Like a pencil pressed against an orbital sander, the ship is shredded to pieces little by little. Bursts of light, explosions, and sparks appear in and around the rapidly deteriorating ship. A trail of metal and bodies follows it downward. A gray and black stain streaks the bright cyclone circling the black hole. Ejected bodies are scattered among the swirling vortex.

Mitsuki is sure she hears a digital, almost robotic, death cry as the ship is torn apart. Thinking it's a glitch in her EBT, she instinctively reaches for it but finds it is gone. She quietly wonders if MAIa was truly self-aware and experienced her destruction.

The angel proclaims, "Humanity thought it could propel itself into the heavens like the Babylonians. In its hubris, much of humankind has forgotten the eternal death; it believes there is no judgment. Man does not see the danger in easy living or in carnal pleasure. Instead, the illicit passions of many were inflamed, exciting them to follow their selfish desires and forsake holiness. Gaze now into the storm and see what becomes of them."

There, they discover more than dust, ice, and debris. The bodies of their fellow crewmembers and millions of additional souls are trapped in the fiery disc. Moisture boils in their shipmates' mouths. They cannot breathe. The remaining gasses in their lungs expand, rupturing them and releasing air bubbles into their boiling bloodstream. Their tissue and skin swell as the water in their bodies vaporizes. Cosmic radiation burns their bloated skin. Deep, excruciating pain in their joints, hips, and spine contorts their naked bodies. Thousands of invisible tiny spiders crawl all over the skin of each soul, cocooning them in foul silk before the heat from the black hole mummifies them.

Though their distorted faces are frozen in anguish, their eyes still move, and their ears hear. Each man and woman searches for relief yet finds none. Their bodies are ravaged by space debris, but each soul is still alive, trapped in agony in its mummified body. Oxygen escaping through their searing throats joins the wave-like wailing heard when the Bab-ilu emerged from the wormhole.

As they search the accretion disc for fellow crewmembers, the two are shocked to find their physical bodies. Still kneeling, their mummified remains are surrounded by three portions of wall from Yared's old quarters. Their lifeless husks are preserved in a state of prayer, their last act aboard the Bab-ilu.

Without turning around, Yared mumbles, "Then we are dead, too?"

"Yes," the angel confirms.

Yared asks, "Why did we not feel such torment and pain?"

"A mercy granted to you because of your faith."

"What of the other poor souls in the disc?" Yared asks

"Most are bound for the black gate, for they rejected Our Blessed Lord. Only a few will find the narrow path."

A second luminous angel, dressed similarly to the first but wearing a cape and hood of pure white and carrying a shield and spear, moves gracefully between Mitsuki and Yared. As he passes, he says, "Follow us."

The two do not hesitate to follow their protectors. The angels lead them safely to a place between the black depths and the white-hot plasma jet. Here, they remain stationary and observe the unfolding scene.

"There," the second angel points his spear toward the black hole. "Your captain leads the way for his crew."

Something unseen drags the once proud Nimbus into the inescapable night of the black hole by his broken ankle. Terror has replaced his facade of pride and arrogance as he flails and grasps for anything to slow his descent. Suddenly, his body emblazes like a torch set on fire. However, the flame is quickly extinguished after he passes through the corona.

Unfortunately for Kieran, time slows as he nears the event horizon, the beginning of eternal pain. His charred, smoking corpse of a body begins to twist and elongate; spaghettification has already started. Bones crack, muscles tear, and seared skin splits open. Kieran's dull gray soul is gradually ripped from his gravity-distorted body. Still clawing at the nothingness of space, his body echoes the scream in desperation delivered up from the core of his soul. His shrieking is eventually silenced as his body and soul slip into total darkness, disappearing forever.

"But for the grace of God, there go I," Yared shutters in horror.

"Indeed," the angel affirms. "Kieran Nimbus thought he was a great admiral, ready to conquer the heavens. He thought himself cunning and invincible; however, he was nothing more than a pawn to the fallen. He has passed beyond the black veil, where there is no tomorrow for those who slip beyond it. He will continue to be pulled downward through fire and chaos, losing more space and time until he finally reaches the singularity. It is a place of crushing darkness and gnashing of teeth. There is no peace on that plane of existence."

Listening to the angel speak, Yared widens his view on the battlefield for souls. He is surprised to see hundreds of Anunnaki moving freely about the asteroids as if it were a galactic ant farm. Suddenly, it strikes him that this place, not Terranaki, is the true colony. The demonic Anunnaki tempt, torment, and abuse human souls captured there until they are harvested and dragged to the black gate. He sees three Anunnaki drones protesting in futility as one angelic being removes a rare soul from the celestial tempest.

Mitsuki also notices this happening around the disk, the tiny handful of believers being separated from it. The blessed few spiral out like a radial arm of the Milky Way. They move steadily along a narrow column on a thin path of what looks like glittering white sand located just above the photon sphere. Much like the two leading her and Yared, a guardian angel escorts each soul on this path.

As she observes the joyful procession, she notices a single soul being diverted from the narrow path and toward them instead. She gasps with excitement, "Aleksandr!"

"Yes, dear one." Her guardian angel assures her, "Our Lord favors those who repent and willingly lay down their lives for their friends."

Though there is no ground to run on, Aleksandr rushes toward his friends as if there were. He greets them with open arms. Embracing Mitsuki and Yared together, he says, "Praise God! KHe saved you."

After the reunion, Yared turns to face their protectors. Always one to think of his crew before himself, he asks, "What is to become of us, mighty one?"

"Yared, it is time for you to see those whom you traveled so far to see, for your destiny lies beyond them." The angel gestures to the Cherubim on either side of the distant and blinding White Gate at the end of the narrow path.

As the angels escort the trio back to the narrow path, Aleksandr boldly asks his protector, "I sought Cherubim vere guardingk Eden?"

"No, Aleksandr, not Eden, but the Tree of Life. They have been vigilant in guarding access to it since the Creator placed them there," his angel responds.

Mitsuki softly adds, "The tree is not in Eden any longer. It grows on the banks of the River of Life now, which flows from the Throne of God and the Lamb."

"Well done, dear one," her angel praises. "You have not forgotten scripture, have you?"

She smiles.

Yared's angel says, "This path leads to life everlasting. As you have already surmised, the world you thought you were being led to, this 'Terranaki,' was false. It was a lie."

Yared asks, "Wait, you were the one who spoke to me in my dream."

"Yes. I am Præsidiel, your guardian."

"Then I must thank you, Præsidiel,"—Yared strikes his breast in salute—"for protecting me even when I did not deserve it."

The angel nods his appreciation before continuing, "You must understand; Terranaki was nothing more than a ghost image installed in your technology by your artificial intelligence. It was pure deception. However, a new world does exist, a new Earth created by Our Heavenly Father. That is where you go."

"So," Aleksandr points to the black hole, "if zhat is Black Gate, zhis is gate to KHeaven?"

His angel answers, "Yes. This is the Purgatorial Gate."

Præsidiel elaborates, "The King of Kings, Our Blessed Lord, sits upon His throne in His new creation. Before entering into His presence, followers of The Way must be purified. Though you have repented and believed, your souls are yet stained with sin. Your impurities must be burned away like gold is purified in fire. This is accomplished after you pass beyond the white veil."

Aleksandr's angel holds out his spear horizontally, stopping them. "Halt and observe."

They watch as three demons in Anunnaki shells attempt a sortie. They intend to draw a handful of the blessed souls away from the narrow path. With spears at the ready, guardian angels keep them at bay. However, one demon spies an opportunity. She motions to the other two, and they fly toward a youthful soul whose foot has slipped off the slender path. They reach for his ankle, hoping to abscond with him.

A fierce roar erupts from one Cherubim's lion face, commanding the flaming sword suspended over the Purgatorial Gate to meet their foes—the sword streaks like a comet through the void toward the demons. It slices cleanly through their exoskeletons, quickly rending each in twain and ending their wicked expedition.

The youthful soul steps back on the twinkling sand, returning to hopeful expectations.

With the sword's mission completed, the Cherubim's eagle face makes a loud screech, commanding the sword to return to its position above the White Gate.

The lifeless husks of Anunnaki demons fall away into the Black Gate.

Aleksandr's guardian lifts his spear, and they continue to advance toward the White Gate.

Forgetting about the galactic phenomenon around him, Yared focuses on the gate in the narrow jet ahead. Alabaster columns adorned with gold and shimmering with a soft pearl hue reach upward, dissipating into the plasma. An archway reaches between them, but only the lower part is visible. A portion of the walls that extended from the columns out to the edge of the plasma jet is visible. Steps lead up to elaborate gates of gold and silver with rounded tops, which open outwardly toward them.

On each side of the open gate stands the fearsome Cherubim. The twelve-foot-tall sentinels stand motionless on either side of the gateway embedded in the plasma jet. Their arms are crossed over their muscular human-shaped torsos. Sturdy oxen legs protrude straight from under their blue tunics. Lined with eyes, their upper wings spread skyward over the archway, the tip of each touching that of the other. Their two lower wings are wrapped around their sides, girding their loins. Each Cherub has a human face in front, a lion's face on the right side, the face of an ox on the left, and an eagle's face on the back.

Each one stands atop a white marble column, which seems to vanish into space at its base. Their flaming sword hangs behind their wings, its fiery tip reaching just below the archway. Their golden color makes them stand out against the dark, star-filled galaxy twinkling in the background; they reflect the pure white emanating from the gateway.

When they set out on the Bab-ilu, Yared and his friends initially expected to be awestruck by a new planet. They fantasized about exploring, building, researching, and discovering a new world. However, that pales in comparison to what they're witnessing here at the galaxy's center. They did not know the true properties of the black hole, nor did they know of the purgatorial gate embedded in the relativistic jets or the majesty of their heavenly guardians. Now, they find themselves approaching the divine.

As they prepare to climb the stairs to the White Gate, Præsidiel reminds them, "All you have ever known is physical space and time. It is time to put material things behind you, detach yourself from creation, and prepare for eternity beyond space and time. In Purgatory, yearnings for material needs will be burned away. When you emerge from the fire, you will enter Our Lord's kingdom with only heavenly desires."

Like a boy staring at a monolithic statue, Aleksandr's mouth gapes open as he looks up with awe at the Cherubim. Mitsuki approaches quietly and humbly, her eyes fixed on what lies beyond the gate. Yared follows them, taking everything in while contemplating seeing 'the way, the truth, and the life' with his own eyes.

It is not surprising when Aleksandr breaks the silence. Raising his hand, he says, "I'll see you on ozher side, *tovarishch*." He turns to his winged guardian, "Sank you, my angel, and praise God, almighty!"

Bold and fearless, the Chief bounds happily through the open gate, his soul vanishing upward in the cleansing white-hot fire.

Mitsuki bows humbly and respectfully to her guardian angel, saying, "*Domo arigato gozaimasu.*" She then turns to her friend and former First Mate, smiling and addressing him by his name for the first time, "See you again soon, Yared-sama."

Yared smiles before she turns and glides through the gate into the jet.

Then, Yared glances over his shoulder, scanning space and time one last time. He's ventured out into the world and on through the cosmos. He has seen amazing things, but he knows nothing is comparable to what he is about to experience. Still, he admires the creator's works one last time. Then, thinking of the marvelous angel who brought him safely here, he turns to Præsidiel and asks, "Will I see you again?"

"Yes, in due time."

"Good. I look forward to it. Thank you."

Præsidiel nods and then lifts his arm, directing Yared toward the gate.

Yared knows the fire will burn. He also knows that it is only temporary. Excitement for seeing Our Lord Jesus swell tenfold in his heart. He smiles as he ascends the steps and enters the purifying white light.

The End

About the Author

John Eudy is a 26-year military veteran. He was a soldier in the Army National Guard and a 'shallow water' sailor in the U.S. Coast Guard.

Admittedly not as well-traveled as the wayfarer rat, he has at least been up and down the river a time or two. Additional expeditions include cautiously wandering the lava fields of Kilauea, snowshoeing to the summit of Cadillac Mountain, strolling among giants in King's Canyon, and swimming with wild dolphins in the Gulf of America (which he embarrassingly thought were sharks at first sight). John even traveled through time once... by making a roundtrip across the international date line to visit Guam.

These days, John and his family reside smack-dab in the middle of the country. He has been married to his lovely wife of 30 years, and they are the proud parents of four daughters, two of whom are already with God in heaven.

Inspired by faith and scripture, he enjoys weaving history, cultural legends, personal life experiences, and Christian morality into fictional novellas.

Other Books by John Eudy

A Glorious Day in Hell:
The Day Jesus Descended

Guardian of the Lightning Seeds

Legacy of Lightning
Rise of the Hotaru Onna-musha

Morning Glories & Moonflowers

the Journey's End

Humble Warrior Tales

www.ingramcontent.com/pod-product-compliance
Lightning Source LLC
Chambersburg PA
CBHW071529100726
47908CB00004B/1334